the
LAST
WINTER

ADRIAN GRIGORE

The Last Winter
Copyright © 2022 by Adrian Grigore

ISBN
978-1-956529-70-8 (Paperback)
978-1-956529-69-2 (eBook)

Translated by Viviane Prager

Adrian Grigore

The Last Winter

To my friends, the researchers

Donation from the author,

A. Grip

04/24/2024

Portland

TABLE OF CONTENTS

PROLOGUE

The time for the old European continent to freeze again slowly but ineluctably came much earlier than scholars had predicted. In our lands everyone was going into a frenzy and panic flared. People were fleeing towns and cities, deserting their apartments where electricity and heating were out of work, and huddled in the villages where they cut down what had been left of the old woods. The youths were moving to warmer countries, for the winters grew longer and bleaker every year and frost conquered the most sheltered of nests. Food and the most basic staples for survival were growing increasingly expensive. On top of it, a strange phenomenon had developed: "destructive induction," as they called it, since no matter where a war was going on around the world, holes and debris were turning up out of the blue in our towns and villages, although the bombs were falling elsewhere, far away. Local authorities were terribly concerned and went on sending out workers with shovels and wheelbarrows to patch the tarmac, but they could not keep up and the holes were multiplying by the day, as there were many wars all over, particularly oil wars. We had no trouble in this respect: oil had become so scarce and costly in our area that one would rarely see a battered car or bus crawling around the holes. Warped covered wagons drawn by famished horses now rolled along the vestiges of roads and highways. Packs of scamps were prowling here and there in search of loot of which there was no shortage, as many people had run away without much care of what they left behind.

Some blamed it on the planet Earth, the slant of whose rotation axis had changed they said bringing about this catastrophic situation. Others believed pollution was responsible, or wars, while the majority would pin the blame on greedy, sleazy politicians who'd bled the country white through taxes to their benefit, yet God alone knew who was to blame and why he visited this punishment on people.

A modest dreamer lived amongst us in those days that still hoped these mishaps could be reversed. He would tell anyone around they must make a clean breast of their errors, identify the real reasons that lay behind them, and stop repeating them. He didn't hate the wrongdoers. He only wanted to make sure they would not fall back into such doings anymore.

His was a trade that everyone despised as useless. He was a researcher. Besides, he had become a nuisance because of his spectacular discovery that many found annoying. He had scientifically demonstrated and experimentally proved that anyone who did wrong in their lives thereby generated negative energy fields that were proportional with the gravity of their deeds. These fields arising from the evil deeds of every individual were adding up into one big malefic field that became devastating once its intensity increased beyond a certain threshold. It threw nature out of balance and was even apt to generate disasters. He had even found a way to annihilate this harmful energy, but this was not easily done. Actually, it was downright impossible most of the time, as it was the perpetrator of a wrong alone that could unravel the noxious field that he or she had given rise to. Provided that they repented of their deeds and never ever did that anymore. But if they made amends and then relapsed, a new much stronger and more destructive negative energy arose.

After working for many years to make this discovery, he came across the same principle put forth in plain terms in an old book a priest had given him. He remained thoughtful for a while. It dawned on him that mankind had grown vulnerable for disregarding the primeval wisdom and science of the nations. Many modern discoveries were commonplace in ancient times. These thoughts became increasingly preoccupying. He yearned to learn that early wisdom, but felt he was unable to come near it. He didn't dare to set out on a new path of knowledge while many empty human dreams and unfulfilled desires were on his mind. He tried to free himself, shake off those burdens one by one.

One day, as our lands lay doomed under yet another long harsh winter, he returned nostalgically to the research institute where he had been employed for a long spell. He thought the time had come for him to make one of his dreams come true—a very simple, even ludicrous desire that had been dogging him for long, a thorn in his flesh that wouldn't let him be.

1

THE MAN'S BOTH HANDS WERE CLINGING to the ellipses of the huge metal atom the builders, impelled as by some sudden pride, had set right from the start on top of Tower B. He had long yearned to touch the giant atom that seemed to have emerged there from a hyperbolization beyond all bounds of fantasy of the small world of particles. The first time he had set eyes on it, it looked as though a royal crown was standing on the tower. It commanded respect and added to the fame of the building that housed an institution the name of which people would only utter hesitatingly. For years he had waited for a chance to find unlocked the heavy metal door to the roof terrace where the atom rose. The watchful guards would never fail to lock it. And when at last he got his chance, as they were mending the insulation on the roof, and the big door lay open in front of him, he'd hardly made two steps towards the atom that a couple of fellows in overalls grabbed him tight and gave him a few punches. He came to in an ambulance that drove him to the nuthouse on grounds he had attempted to jump off the tower. He tried to tell the hospital people he had never ever thought of killing himself, but they would not believe him. They retained him for a few days and didn't let him go until he'd signed a statement that he would never again climb on the roof of Tower B.

He had once tried to take a close-up of the atom with a telephoto lens, but all he'd got was yet more punches on the scruff from a furious sturdy fellow that turned up suddenly before him, snatched the camera, and dashed it to pieces. He was then dragged to a ground floor room in Tower B where that angry guy's bosses took over and pestered him with questions for several hours. They even made him write so long that his hand ached on sundry subjects that had nothing to do with the fact that he was simply keen on putting on his desk a picture of the unmitigated splendor of the atom crowning Tower B.

The times had changed. Tower B, a shadow of its former self, was just another useless, empty hulk of a building, of which there were so many. The terrace door was no longer locked and this meant a lot to him, as he was now able to do what he had wished to do for so long: he was free to climb on the roof, take a close look and feel the big ellipses of the atom he up to then had only contemplated from afar.

He couldn't help being disappointed: all that was left of the resplendent structure that used to take his breath away was nothing but a maze of rusty limbs, through which the northern wind blew bitterly, whipping his face with furious icy needles. The gusts had swept his cap off and tossed it among the vent holes to the other end of the terrace. His hands were freezing on the metal coils, but he didn't mind: he felt important. From there he had a chance to look down on the surrounding cracked, stripped buildings, from the roofs of which the wind was pulling tin strips that rolled around in clatter.

Eyes closed, he tried to imagine how all this would have looked decades ago when everything was new and freshly painted. He recalled that on the front lawn outside Tower B there used to be a sort of pendant of the upper symbol—an atom made of evergreens and brightly colored flowers. The previous summer, he'd seen a peasant tie up his cow on that spot and now he wondered whether the shrubby atom was still there. He leaned over the railing and looked down at the lawn on which sparse flakes were beginning to set. It wasn't. All that remained was a few bushes on a waste ground strewn with gaping potholes, as though the shrubs had been plucked out in haste, stolen perhaps. It took quite some imagination to figure that there used to be a flowerbed with perfect geometric lines down there. Some stray dogs had taken shelter among the few remaining bushes. Right in the middle where once the nucleus of plants had been the animals had dug a sort of burrow. All around it the ground was littered with plastic bags in which some charitable soul had brought them bones and drab lumps of polenta.

A covered wagon had pulled up in front of the tower. Nearby, a bunch of shaggy mustached gypsies were pressing on a lever trying to pry out of the asphalt a manhole cover that wouldn't budge. One of the men fetched a sledgehammer from the wagon and started banging on the cover, but the thick lid resisted and after every blow, as if crying for help, let out a kind of wail that drew loud echoes from the tower walls. Encircling the group, the dogs barked rabidly, but the busy men paid no notice: they only cared about their task. Up on the building, he thought he should perhaps yell at them, warn them that they were doing something wrong. Stealing the sewer cover just outside Tower B in broad daylight was sheer insolence. He wondered where the hell were the tower guards that they didn't hear or see those bums stealing under their very nose, but he remembered that the doors were locked and it had been a long time no one guarded the building anymore. He himself was an intruder, since he had sneaked inside through a broken basement window.

He let the gypsies go on with their job untroubled and, as his ears were freezing, walked over to pick up his cap from where the wind had swept it. Suddenly a fresh gust blinded him with snow and staggering he lost direction. When he could see again a moment later, he was leaning on the southern railing. Down in the backyard alley between the pavilions there was a bustle going on. Some people were unloading sacks from trucks, probably feed. The new owner who'd won the auction when everything went on the block had set up a poultry farm.

He shook the snow off his cap, stood gazing at the atom for a few instants, and said to himself it was time to go. He was cold and disappointed. Coming close at last to the symbol that had mesmerized him for so long did not at all take place as he'd expected. He climbed down and carefully closed the heavy metal door behind him. Countless times he had stood in frustration before that terrace door, shaking it stubbornly, but it never opened and put off the materialization of a dream for just too long.

On the last story the blizzard had wiped in snow through a window that did not close and water dripping from a broken radiator had turned the hallway floor linoleum into a skating rink. Leaning on the wall, he treaded carefully up to the stairway balustrade. He should have taken the other side of the corridor, the way he had climbed up. The floor there wasn't slippery at least. Someone had ripped off the linoleum, but the dried glue had obstinately stuck to the concrete forming an antiskid surface.

On his way down he stopped before the metal frame where the most important door in Tower B once stood. It led to a very special area—the big boss' secretary's office. It was there that the selection was made, that the decision was taken on whether one could see the chairman or was just in for a long wait. After much begging and pleading, the timid, vaguely hopeful petitioner was allowed to open the red padded door behind which sat the chairman on his throne, a sultan that could make or break the fortune of any of his subjects, which he did depending on his whims or on the graft and connections of those that reached to see his face.

The empty secretary's office was a shambles and the red padded door was gone, only the oaken doorposts were still standing. Too bad, he would have liked to count the padding nails again. He had counted them so many times while waiting for an audience that he began to sort of fancy it. It was a test: there were lots of small tacks, besides many of the heads were missing, so it took a keen eye to detect them.

In a corner of the room, mice were rollicking on a pile of papers. A cabinet with a broken glass pane and a dusty desk hardly suggested this once had been the office of a man that reigned over a kingdom of researchers. He took a close look at the armchair and realized it was the same: it was the chairman's black leather chair all right. Wiping off the dust, he sat down cautiously on the edge because the back was barely holding by one nail. He looked warily around as though in fear someone might suddenly turn up and expose him as a usurper for sitting—how dared he?—on that important chair. He relaxed slowly, got accustomed to it, even felt like he was entitled to rest in the seat of the very man that once played with his fate and those of a few thousand others.

The daylight peering through the blurred windows was growing dimmer. He thought he'd better go before the night fell: it was a long way to his place and he would have to walk. Yet something seemed to hold him back. He felt he would just stay a little longer. The room was cold; the wind rattled the windows, and a rumble like the sound of an organ came in from the hallways. He fancied hearing the morning buzz of employees coming to work. But how could they have entered—the door was locked. "The basement window, this must be it," he answered his own question in a way that soothed his qualms about breaking in like a burglar—everyone else did. His eyes fell on a switch: he should turn on the light, he thought, but from the center of the ceiling where once the chandelier had been only a tangle of ragged wires hung like empty guts.

The cold was creeping into his body stealthily at first, as a mere impression, then more and more aggressively. He hunched up in the chair, drawing his arms across his chest to warm up. It must have been the visit to the roof that chilled him to the bone. He should start moving rather than just sit there in the chairman's seat and let himself freeze stiff. A cheeky mouse sneaking up his shoulder finally prompted him to stand up. Time to go.

The tower's corridors were dark now and he could hardly see his way, but he set off nevertheless. Feeling around and clinging to the banisters, he started to climb down counting the floors, trying to recognize the places where once the offices, conference rooms, and library had been.

A heap of rubble that blocked the stairs on the fourth floor made him go back around the elevators shaft to find the other stairway. He passed a door wide open. In the scant light that peered from outside he saw a jumble of shelves piled up on top of one another while lots of books littered the floor. His presence scared the pigeons that had nested there. They flew up in a flutter of wings and dashed out an open window the pane of which was swinging in the wind. A gust of snow burst in behind them. He stooped and picked up the first book lying in his way. He squinted to discern the title and flew into a rage so high that he could sense something was wrong with him as if a cloud was wrapping up his mind.

"How can they do a thing like that?" he cried out. "A book so valuable lying on the floor! How sloppy can these librarians be? Where have they gone now leaving all this mess?"

He went out into the corridor and yelled:

"Hey, ladies of the library, where are you? Hey, you've got readers waiting. Are you loafing about over your godforsaken coffees yet again?"

His angry voice rebounded on the hallways, quickly overwhelmed by the wailing wind that gushed out of the stairwell. As he was shouting out again, a plaintive mew replied and a pitch-black tomcat came up rubbing against his boots and trouser cuffs. It was his old friend Isaac that staunchly guarded the library against mice and had meanwhile become the guard of the entire tower. Judging by his plump appearance, one could see he was doing fine, except he was terribly lonesome and from then on would escort his freshly rediscovered friend inseparably.

"Say, Isaac, old boy, where are the library ladies?" he asked as he bent down to pat him amicably on the back. You tell me where is everybody in this tower. I see no one comes to work no more. What's going on? Is it all over here?"

Isaac who seemed to understand the question mewed sadly in reply.

"But they don't give a damn of course, do they? They've wrecked it all up! Right now I'm gonna have it out with them. They can't go on like this. It's sheer mockery!"

He set out furiously, gripping the book, with the black cat hopping behind him and mewing all the time, as though he wanted to persuade him not to report the ladies of the library. It was none of their fault: somebody else had made the rules deciding to let the tower go to seed. It was dark on the stairway. Enraged, he rushed down headlong, stumbled, rolled over several times, and banged his forehead on a step.

* * *

He had fallen in the dust of the road and was now wriggling like a trampled worm under the parching sun. His knotty staff, which had bounced off his hand, was lying a few steps away near the empty bag which, soiled with dust, looked like a rag a hurried passer-by would throw away. He tried unsuccessfully to stand up and trudge into the shade of a shrub that still kept on a few leaves spared by the caterpillars.

The hot air whirled along the road like water bursting through a dam trying to flood the earth. He was alone and there was no one in sight that could come up and help him. Like a baby that can't walk yet he crawled on all fours to the roadside and collapsed heavily under a shady eucalyptus.

A moment later, he reopened his eyes in time to see far up the road that twisted among reddish hills, a shaft of dust or smoke that seemed to be storming his way. It looked like a mad dragon with in the middle of the forehead sort of a bright fisheye that sparkled dazzlingly in the sun. Shading his eyes with his hand, he squinted intently trying to make out what it was. Then suddenly he heard a voice behind him with a deep sound like it was rising from the bottom of a well.

"Is that you the researcher faltering at the turn of the century that has become the mockery of fools? Are you the sage that has been bashed and kicked out of the city tower?"

He turned to see who was talking, but there was no one there and, frightened, he kept silent not knowing what, if anything, he was supposed to say.

"Fear not!" the voice went on. "Get up, shake the dust off your clothes, straighten your girdle, and fortify your spirit. He that is coming with great pump down the Chaldeans Road is the Prince of Rosh and lies, Gog and Magog, to whom your enemies have plotted to surrender you. He will tempt you with presents and sweet talk. Don't bow to him, or he will put the sign of the beast onto your forehead."

All of a sudden, every pain in his body melted away and he felt slender and young again. He shook the road dust off his camelhair clothes with both hands, picked up his bag and hung it proudly on his shoulder, grasped his staff, but all along his eyes were riveted on the dust whirl that was drawing near.

Riding ahead was a warrior clad in a bright silver armor, over which a crimson mantle floated in the wind. The ostrich-feathered helmet made him look taller than he was, but as the rider pulled back the horse in front of him, he noticed there was no head beneath the helmet: it simply hung up in the air above the armor. He stared at that bizarre thing in astonishment and couldn't believe his eyes. He realized there was no warrior in the armor either: the silver hull stuck on the saddle was empty but for a few tan bones that showed up at the joints.

A herd of bulls came clattering behind him. They stopped and began bellowing, shaking their horns, and routing in the dust.

"You needn't be surprised," the voice explained. "The Prince of Rosh died long ago, but his restive spirit keeps roaming in the wilderness sowing death and destruction. He's heading for Nineveh right now. Follow him!"

"Why should I trail this evil-breeding spirit?" he wondered in perplexity. "What am I to do in the city of Nineveh?"

"Go there and save the tablets on which the early science and wisdom of the peoples are inscribed!" the voice urged. "Nineveh will soon be destroyed for the sins of its residents, but the tablets in its library must endure and enlighten those to come. Rescue them! This is the commandment!"

"I'm just a poor researcher all by myself and helpless," he ventured to say while trying to figure out where the voice came from. "How could I fulfill such a commandment? I can easily be caught and flung into jail or even killed."

"Everything will be fulfilled as ordained and you will prevail provided that you keep in the right path. Beware of the temptations of all kinds that will beset you. Above all, beware of giving in to despair or slipping into pride, for either one will be the end of you."

"What about these bulls that bellow fearfully and rout the dust? Who is their master? How come they wander in the wilderness and how can they be managed?" he asked again, increasingly confused, still peeking around unable to locate the secret voice.

"They are your army. With their mighty horns they will knock down any obstacle standing in your way and their bellows will terrify your enemies."

That was all he could hear, as a strong whirlwind suddenly arose that swept him from the ground and hurled him among the horns of the bulls. The herd set into motion and he found himself on a bull's back riding behind the silver armored warrior that galloped proudly, spear in hand, along the twisting path, known as the Chaldeans Road, that led across the Euphrates and on to the great city of Nineveh, on the banks of the Tigris.

They rode across a valley watered by a clear brook. The bulls were thirsty. They slowed down and were about to stop and drink when the silver-clad rider thrust his spear into the water and it turned into blood. The animals, for all their thirst, would have none of it. They moved on.

The night had fallen. The sun was hiding beyond the rocks and a cool breeze blew. He would have liked to call a halt and camp, but no one would listen to him in that tumult. The warrior kept riding resolutely and the herd followed him in submission, rocking the earth beneath their hoofs. Suddenly, he was snatched up in the air again and put down by the road under a palm tree. As he was struggling back to consciousness, he thought he heard someone saying:

"He isn't dead, just sunstruck. Give him some water and he'll be all right. Go fetch the skin from the donkey's back!"

No sooner had he felt the jar pressing his lips than he gulped greedily a few drafts and felt as though a cloud suddenly lifted from his mind. He was lying between two shepherds who'd found him on the road and had him carried on their donkey to the valley where they had their cave. The two were leaning over him and when they saw him open his eyes and drink, they were as happy as if a lamb was born to their herd.

"Bless the Lord my God who has entrusted me to you and not to robbers," he said as he sat up.

"Bless yourself, stranger!" they replied and handed him another full jar.

He grasped it with both hands and sat down on a boulder to drink at leisure. In the grass at his feet a cricket had sneaked out from some crevice and filled the valley with his chirp. He thought the cricket was perhaps thirsty too, so he dropped a little water in his palm and spread it gently on the dry grass blades trying to make it look like dew. He waited vainly: the small bug, busy with its chirping, would not drink. Then he saw a lizard crawling out of the rock. Its tongues were out like needles and its open mouth seemed dry. This one must be thirsty indeed. He poured another drop in his hand and held it out for the reptile, but the lizard took fright and hid in the grass. The shepherds looked at him in astonishment and the younger of them who had a short curly beard, chided him:

"Stop wasting the water, brother! We have great trouble carrying it in skins from distant places. We've offered it to you that you can drink, not throw it in the grass. Stop sharing with the crawling beasts and crooners of the night what we have given you because we found you weak and thirsty, fallen in the dust."

"My thirst can wait," he retorted curtly as he held out the jar. "Take it back. I didn't ask for any water. You offered it to me, but if you need it, take it, pour it back into the skin, and let it slake someone thirstier than I."

"You have a strange, proud way of talking, stranger," the older shepherd said chidingly and leaned forth on his staff to give him a close scrutiny. "Where are you from?"

"I'm from a country many days' walk from here."

"Yet you speak our language well and dress the same way as we do," the shepherd said wonderingly. "So whereto are you heading? And how come you passed out on the road?"

"I'm going to the city of Nineveh and I collapsed because I'm worn out and my victuals are all gone. Robbers could have killed me or the beasts of the wilderness could have ripped my flesh, but the Lord my God, who did not forsake me, did not let it happen."

"Who is your God and how do you fulfill his will? What sort of offerings do you present to him?" the shepherd sounded him out.

"The Lord my God is He who created the heavens and the earth, and everything we see, and everything we don't see, but is nevertheless. I kill no lambs or fattened rams to burn for Him. I do the will of the Lord in a way you might find hard to grasp."

"How's that? By watering the beasts that move along the ground and bugs that croon by night?" the younger shepherd scoffed.

"They, too, are creatures fated to live with us."

The shepherds looked at each other in astonishment. They had never heard anyone talk like that. Then, as the sheep had scattered all over the field and the night was flowing out untrammeled from the steep banks of the valley, they went to round the flock up and put it to shelter under guard of the dogs. He remained sitting on the boulder outside the cave that was the shepherds' home, jar still in hand, eyes wandering across the field, as he tried to make out where he was and how long he would still have to walk to Nineveh.

The cool breeze of the night ruffled his locks and the bushy beard that covered his suntanned emaciated cheeks. The luminaries of the night were mounting on the firmament. The moon had risen from between two cliffs painting the skies blood red. Every now and then stray clouds drifting by from above the sea were shading her face.

The shepherds lit a fire before the cave and spread a towel on the grass. They put on it three pitas and salt meat toasted over the cinders, and bade him help himself. He did and took himself a piece of bread but didn't touch the meat.

Hungry after the day's chores, the two were wolfing down big chunks of meat the fat of which was dripping through their fingers. At first, they paid no notice to him, but finally they realized he shunned the juicy meat they browned over the fire and bade him once again to eat. Immersed in idle contemplation of the valley, he did not answer.

"Why aren't you eating any meat? Don't worry: there's plenty of it for us all," the older shepherd said, wiping his greasy hands on a dry tuft of grass and pouring water from the skin into his palm to wash down the salty meat.

"I am forbidden to eat any creature that flies, or crawls along the ground, or moves on it lest I defile my body," he replied.

"Do you mean to say that we defile ourselves by eating off the work of our hands and from the flock we tend?"

"You heard me right. Whenever you eat out of an animal you killed for food, you defile yourself and sin, as you have taken a life, for no one is the master of life except the Lord my God."

"I don't dig it, stranger," the younger shepherd joined in angrily. "Why shan't we eat off our flock? Shall we give up the rules of yore that our elders and wise men have handed down to us? What would you have us eat? The dust of the road?"

"By no means, my friend," the stranger said soothingly. "Let me explain it to you. The earth the Lord my God has given us to rule upon is full of fruit and grain that nurture life as oil nurtures light in a lamp. In truth I'm telling you we have not been put on this earth to gorge our bellies but rather to keep and honor the old laws and live in peace and justice with our neighbors."

"Look, stranger, I know nothing of your laws, but ours do not keep us from any joy of the flesh, least of all from feasting or making merry or relishing on the broiled calves and rams of our folds."

"You're right about you keeping your own laws, but have you ever wondered if he who gave you these laws really knew how to protect you from the danger of letting loose the cravings of the body lest they might turn you all into the likes of beasts?"

"Hey, there!" the younger shepherd cried out in a threatening voice. "Do you mean that we are unclean and will end up like the wild beasts if we observe our commandments and keep the rules the ancient sages of our people have handed down to us?"

"Easy, lad! Don't let the darkness get hold of your mind," he cut in gently. "To make sure that you get my point and find out for yourself what dangers are out there in store for us, please listen carefully to what I will disclose to you. Some things we don't know only because we do not want to know them, and when we learn them we'd rather not believe them because we do not want or cannot understand them. Everything that has happened up to now and that will happen in the world the wise men had it all written down in ancient times. Their writ has been preserved with utmost care so that the peoples be enlightened and grope no longer in the dark. Those who are wise and resolute enough to grasp the meaning of these writings can see in them as in a mirror how this world began and what its end will be."

"The end? What do you mean?" the younger shepherd asked in surprise. "Will there be an end to the world? Is it going to perish?"

"That's right, my friend. The world had a beginning and will have an end, same as a river starts from a spring in the mountains and finally flows into the vast sea."

The shepherds seemed to have forgotten all about their meaty spits sizzling over the cinders, as they sat hanging on his lips. The moon was up two spears above the peaks. The flock was sleeping peacefully in the valley and the dogs, too, were quiet and drowsy. The crickets alone seemed to be out of every crack of the earth and chorused making the valley whiz. The wind was growing stronger and sometimes rushed through the quiet dinner before the cave sweeping away the cinders.

He suddenly stood up and raised his hands to the sky:

"Do you like the moon that shines at night so you don't have to fumble in the dark and lose your sheep? Do you like this starry sky, this wind that gently cools your faces? Do you like this valley where you live your lives and the brooks that flow among the cedars in the mountains where you often take your flocks? Well, there once was none of these. Nothing that we now see existed. Darkness was everywhere and the earth was empty and in disarray. Everything was created through the Word of God. The earth was tidied up, wisely bedight, and given to us, humans, to rule over, but we are wicked and ungrateful. We drift away from knowledge even as we brag about how wise we are. We think we're building, but are tearing down. We wish to live long but are shortening our days through vain delights. The human kind is like a host of caterpillars that gnaw away the leaves of the trees and never bother to think the master of the orchard will grow angry when he finds no fruit to gather. For it is written: When the end of the age comes, there will be signs; there will be great floods and earthquakes that will bring down the mountains. Fearful winds and rains of fire will sweep over the earth so deeply that even for the fish down on the bottom of the sea there will be no escape."

The shepherds listened to him in bewilderment and wondered whether he was indeed a sage or a lunatic roaming in the wilderness. The younger one thought he might try to taunt him.

"Master," said he, "methinks you speak like a wise man and, if I get you right, you know the ancient secrets of the earth, so could you clarify one thing for me?"

"Ask your question and, if I can, I will enlighten you," he replied.

"How come it is only we, humans, that must observe laws and commandments? Can it be that the animals we rule over are actually our betters since they don't need to obey any laws, nor keep any commandments, and still live?"

"If your question, my friend, springs out of ignorance, let your mind be enlightened, and if it springs from pride or mockery, let your spirit feel the pangs of remorse. Listen to me! Nothing moves unless it is commanded to do so and no creature that disobeys commandments goes unpunished. I'm telling you the truth. Before the Lord my God made man the master of the earth, He ordered by His Word that everything useful to life should be made ready. Warm rain fell on the earth and mild winds blew and sweet grass grew and covered up the fields so that fresh verdure basking in the sunlight was everywhere you looked. And if a seed fell on the ground, within a few days a tree grew there and bore fruit. And the Lord my God then created living creatures for the water and air and land, useful animals and wild animals, according to their kinds, and ordered them to feed on grass and be fruitful, and fill the earth. Many of them were huge, fearful beasts, which yet obeyed the commandments they had been given. They filled valleys and mountains, fields and forests, eating nothing but greenery and drinking from the clear brooks of the earth. Then the Lord's command went into disregard and many of those beasts would no longer eat green plants and began to test their fangs on the flesh of fellow animals. The evil spirits that unseen by us humans haunt the earth and hatefully hover above every creature of the Lord slipped artfully into those animals and incited them to eat one another although there was plenty of grass to go around. Soon enough, horrible predators with bloodshot eyes and pointed teeth and claws were prowling all over the earth and mangling every living creature in their way. The Lord my God was incensed seeing His creatures, work of His hands, fall into disobedience, kill, and prey on one another. He visited his wrath on them and all the big frightening beasts died and rot spreading a terrible stench. The black fluid they draw out of wells along the valleys of Mesopotamia and which many people use to grease their chariot wheels with, may well be the fat of those disobedient creatures.

The shepherds, who were listening to him in awe, were beginning to think that perhaps the man that stood before them was really a wise man and indeed knew the ancient secrets of the earth.

"Where did you learn all these things?" the older shepherd dared to ask. "Did the ancient sages of the peoples put them down in writing, as you said?"

"They did and everything was written on divine command, as it was written that we, humans, were made of dust, that the earth was put under our rule, and that we were commanded to be fruitful and observe the law. Yet the cunning evil spirits that haunt the world hang spitefully above us and egg us on to mischief."

"Deep is your wisdom, master," said the younger shepherd who felt sorry for the arrogant question he had asked. "But since you mentioned the unclean spirits tailing us and driving us to evil, could you tell me where they come from and why are they often stronger than us humans?"

His eyes now wandered around the valley on which the moon was shedding its pale light. He didn't answer any longer.

"I'll go find myself a place to sleep in the grass down there. I'll be on my way to Nineveh at dawn," he said at last. "May you be rewarded for all the trouble that you took with me today and may the food and water that we gave me be received as an offering. Blessed be your labor and may your flocks be fruitful and gratify your masters and your kin."

The shepherds were at a loss to match the stranger's blessings, so they just handed him a camelhair blanket to lie on, while the two of them, tired, leaned back against two boulders each on one side of the cave mouth, shaded their eyes with their hands against the moonlight, and presently were fast asleep.

The stranger walked away, passed by the sleeping flock without waking the dogs, and found himself a hollow in the rock in which he spread his blanket for the night. He looked up searching for the east and, hands raised towards the starry vault, stood motionless a long time like a stone.

The wind was blowing stronger than before, ruffling his woolly beard and unkempt locks. The moonlight made the shadows of his lifted arms look like a pair of tongs clasping the valley.

Once he finished his prayer, he lied down between the rocks and tried to sleep, but then there was a rumble and a nacreous steam rose from the cracks in the ground, encircling him and dancing in the moonlight, while squeaky voices began nagging him, urging him to go kill the shepherds and steal their flock. He stood up and scolded them:

"Curse be upon you and your masters, dark spirits of the earth!" he spoke out loud.

Swept by the wind, the steam that whirled around him was sucked back into the ground, rumbling like a pot boiling on the fire. The dogs started in fright and began to bark and howl filling the valley with their clatter.

*   *   *

He lay on the cold concrete at the foot of the stairs, his hand still gripping the book that he had picked up from the messy library. He kept hearing the howl of the dogs. There must have been a lot of them by now prowling around the tower like a hungry pack of wolves. He stood on his knees and still holding the book started to climb up, leaning on the banisters. All of a sudden he felt strange: the book seemed to be burning in his palm like a red-hot brick. Then words came sparking out of its pages. They didn't look like ink black outlines, as you'd expect them to, but rather like some kind of glow-worms that were surrounding him, hurting his eyes, while he just stood there not knowing what to do or how to protect himself. He felt that pages full of heavy formulas he'd always wanted unsuccessfully to learn by heart were cramming into his brain while droves of others buzzed furiously like wasps around his head.

The cat was mewling like a beaten baby. He vaguely heard the broken sounds and thought he might have hurt the poor beast in his fall. He turned around looking for him, but saw a gentleman in a fine black suit walking up instead of the cat. The gentleman caught up with him, patted his shoulder, and affably offered his help for he had seen him limp. No, thanks, it wasn't serious, he was fine, he said, while he kept asking himself how the smart gentleman that used to hold a mighty important post in Tower B had suddenly turned up. As they arrived at the next floor, the man in black fiddled a moment with the switch and a mild, cozy light went on, so he was now able to see quite well what was going on up there. Oddly enough, the corridor was in a bustle and he could even spot some of his lab mates, but they seemed to avoid him and vanished swiftly round a corner.

"Thank god they've finally showed up to work," he said with some sympathy turning to the gentleman in black. "There was no one here when I climbed down a little earlier. The tower was all locked up and empty like it had been closed down for good."

Then, as he knew the gentleman was always well informed, he thought he might as well ask a delicate question:

"Do you happen to know whether they've come upon some funding source for our research projects? Are they going to give us our back pay?"

The man just mumbled something that he couldn't make out, but he hadn't paid much attention to the answer anyway. He had stopped staring at the chairman's office door, astonished to see it back in the old metal frame so quickly and everything looking again the way it used to be. The gentleman in black suddenly talked to him and quite clearly this time:

"Have you registered for an audience with comrade chairman?"

"Yeah, sort of," he answered hesitatingly.

"If you have any personal problem, I might be able to help. I'm his adviser, you know."

He walked in and saw the chairman's same secretary that he'd known for a long time. So she had not retired, as they told him, after all. She was still there, rattling the typewriter like a machinegun. Maybe he ought to tell her times have changed, he thought. Why toil on the old typewriter when a PC and printer would make her job so much more comfortable? He told her nothing, though, for she looked too absorbed in whatever paper she was writing, to even notice him. When she was done with it, she scowled at him askance and blurted out:

"It's you again? I've told you he will not see you, haven't I? Do you think comrade chairman has the time to talk with every crackpot? Buzz off, will you!"

She rolled the letter out and promptly vanished behind the padded door into the chairman's den. Confused, he turned to the black-suited gentleman, trying to justify his presence.

"It's not for my own sake this time, you know. About that trip abroad, I got the point, won't press for it. It's something else that cannot be delayed. The library's a shambles. They don't even have windows any more, or shelves— the books are all scattered on the floor. Look what's become of this book—such a mess— It's a shame. Listen to me—I know what I'm talking about—this is the paramount book of every physicist."

He held it out to show him, but the man gave him a nonplussed stare and grumbled:

"Come on, comrade! This is but a plain piece of board. This is no book!"

"I beg your pardon! You clearly know nothing about physics, do you?" he said, pushing the thing yet closer to the man's nose. "This is just the material side, the wood they made the paper of for printing. The scientific contents, I've saved it in my brain for now, but people ought to be informed about this book, for it has suffered an involution, look at it, I mean it has reverted to its raw material state. This is what the entire library will come to:

it will all turn into a wood store. The contents need to be rescued presently. Every researcher has a duty to save at least one book by memorizing it, as I did.

"Well, sure, why not?" the other muttered and off he went, while he stood there, pressing the board beneath his arm, and waited for the secretary to come back.

When she finally did and found him still there, she snapped at him angrily:

"Stop wasting your time, comrade. If they denied you the approval, then that's that. Do you think going abroad is just for fun? With your record, there's nothing more to talk about. The case is closed. You'll never be allowed to travel! Not even to a Socialist country!"

"Please, just a minute, please! You're getting it all wrong. This is not about my going to that conference to which I was invited. It's something else. I must report a serious situation. The library has started to degenerate. Steps must be taken presently. See for yourself!" he said, showing the piece of wood to her. "Here is the proof! This used to be a book and not just any book, but a rare one. On quantum theory—"

"Man, you're even crazier than I thought. We'll have to deal with it once more and put you back where you belong! I'm going to inform myself those who should know about it that they can send a car here right away."

She resolutely picked up the phone and talked to someone, telling them who she was and what she wanted, while he just stood by the door not understanding zilch. Two husky fellows shortly afterward came in and he remembered seeing them during one of those "welcome-home" actions when people were being taken to the airport to meet the president back from some foreign visit. He knew that they were coming for him and, to avert any more thrashing, he meekly followed them out of the room. Once in the corridor, however, he found himself alone again. Right then, the gentleman in black holding a bulky folder in his hand passed him by and greeted him courteously, as though they hadn't met for a long time. A few steps on, he turned and told him in a friendly voice:

"Comrade, I've pondered on your problem and I think we can work it out. I'll make a report to the chairman. Look, I might even talk to him right now. I'm going in to brief him on some matters anyway. Wait outside. I'll call you in if necessary."

He remained in the corridor. He dared not go into the secretariat again lest those two fellows came back for him and beat him up this time. He hoped the man in black would turn the chairman round to see him and he was sorry he hadn't brought along that paper of his that had stirred up such an uproar in other countries. He could have showed it to the chairman. All of a sudden, the board began to stir intensely and a boiling wood stench was spilling from beneath his arm. He had hardly started to consider this phenomenon that some hot fluid similar to lava gushed out of his brain and flowed along his arm and palm and fingers. The board snapped into hundreds of splinters that broadened, lengthened, smoothened, and piled up nicely back beneath his arm except for a few sheets that were still frantically looking for their place.

The next thing he knew, the secretary was shoving him into the office where the black-clad gentleman was making broad gestures and whispering something to the chairman. He stayed near the door preparing to reply in case they asked him any question. The chairman seemed quite agitated; he had of course so many other problems, especially with a black phone that shrilled every two minutes. With the receiver pressed on his ear, he jumped up at attention every time, saying, "Yes, comrade, I understand," while it was obvious from his face that he disliked whatever he was hearing. In between these conversations, he yelled at the black-suited man, calling him an incompetent and threatening to sack him on the spot, but the other didn't seem to care and went on with his low-voice explanations. Finally, the man in black pointed at him as he was standing by the door. He gathered that his case had been brought up, but as the chairman put his glasses on and saw whom this was all about, he roared:

"What's gotten into you, you, stupid prick, bringing this raving lunatic again into my office? Take him the fucking out of here. Take him to the nuthouse and leave him there!"

"Please, comrade chairman, let me explain it to you. The comrade has made a discovery that they are making quite a fuss about abroad. A foreign government official personally invited him to that conference—"

"So what? What's the big deal, turning around those atoms, as they do, like pigs rolling a pumpkin in the yard?"

"It is important that we find a way," the gentleman in black pressed on. "Our country's reputation is at stake."

"OK, I got your point, man. But go ahead; tell me how will you send this wacko out there? It can't be done and you know fucking well it can't. You want the party big shots kick my ass? Look at this asshole! Will we allow him to make fools of us?"

"Who said anything about sending him out there? I think I've found a way to get us all out of this jam—if you agree, of course."

"Let's see! Come out with it! I know that's plenty of monkey business in your skull."

"Well, it's easy. You see, the comrade has just decided to send a letter to those gentlemen out there, tell them his poor health will prevent him from attending, but would they please agree that a younger fellow researcher go instead?"

"Yeah, that's better!" the chairman muttered. "Who do you think should go?"

"You know," the man in black said with a sly smile.

"Oh, I see!" the chairman said all lightened up, adding as though with preternatural conviction: "Of course, this is the best thing we can do. Have him sign that letter."

He didn't understand what letter they were talking about. The black-suited advisor gestured him to a seat at a small table where the chairman usually entertained his guests. Then he pulled out from his black suit a typed sheet of paper and a ballpoint pen and showed him where to put his signature.

He looked across the neatly typed text and felt that he was choking. He had hardly gasped a few words to show his disapproval that the advisor furiously seized him by the collar and whispered seethingly:

"Fuck you, you, piece of shit! What do you think you're doing? Sign it, or else I'll see you rot in a straitjacket. D'you hear me?"

"No, I won't sign it" he resisted, trying to rise and bolt out of the room, but the man in black had grasped his shoulders in his claws and pushed him down.

He startled and woke up in a dark cold place. Isaac, the cat, was mewing, pressing his head against his ribs. He walked out into the snowstorm and the wind cut his face. He wondered whether the two shepherds had safely put their sheep away. He was sorry he'd left without a word of caution. He should have warned them that the man in black was cunning and could steal their flock and that the dogs that howled around the tower were so starved they could turn into ravenous wolves. He felt all mixed-up. Something he couldn't comprehend was happening to him.

2

HE HAD A TERRIBLE HEADACHE, BUT he suspected his tumbling down the stairs was not responsible for it or his hallucinations either. They had been happening for some time. Apparently since they had taken him to mental hospital and shot those doubtful things into his body. It had all started when he would not take part in sorting out potatoes at the railroad station, because he was fed up with simply being out there in the cold and filth and stench all day. A huge mound of potatoes full of slime were rotting at the station and the district party bureau had ordered the institute to take care of it by, as they termed it, patriotic work.

He'd put this straight to his boss he wouldn't go sort out any potatoes for he was a researcher, not a farmer. Had he wanted to be a farmer, he would have stayed back in his native village and become some local big shot, perhaps even the manager of the collective farm. His boss was pissed, but let him be, as the lab claimed credit for his papers every time big bosses at the Science Council were briefing Ceausescu on the physicists' "achievemints."

It was that good-for-nothing squirt from the factory lathing shop that started all the trouble. He'd landed himself some small-time party assignments, so he turned up at the lab waving a sheaf of papers, which he said were a record of how every "workingman" at the institute fulfilled their party duties, which they apparently didn't, as he went on ranting. "These researchers of yours do not respond to party calls," he yelled at the lab head, clearly not giving a damn about the other being considerably older, never mind wiser than he was.

"Your researchers, comrade, are fooling around with the party! At the sports festival only a handful showed up at the stadium to cheer our leaders from the stands. Not to mention the 23rd of August parade or the welcoming actions at the airport—token participation, nothing more! They wouldn't even come boat rowing on the Dambovita when the river project was completed and we were called to celebrate. And, mind you, that was an easy thing to do, a pleasure even! Now, this potato-sorting task the party district has assigned to us—I gather that the comrade researchers are playing hooky once again. I don't care if they're good at research; their political consciousness is low. How can we build Socialist society with such comrades? Such elements shall not be tolerated indefinitely!"

He was supposed to work on a laser alignment job, but this harangue made him fly off the handle. He dropped what he was doing, went up to the squirt and uttered loud and clearly to his face:

"Listen to me, you slob! How dare you talk to us this way? Over here we were building lasers, publishing papers in the topmost journals while you were sucking at your mother's tits! Get the hell out of here, go to your workplace, do some decent work!"

The squirt was stunned to see himself assailed in his capacity as an envoy of the party. His face turned yellowish and he rushed stammering something to the door. Once outside, he went off crying like mad for the police and Securitate to come and nail the reactionary.

Glancing around at his lab colleagues he could read worse than fear on their faces. They knew what was they'd be put through after this. There will be lengthy statements they will have to write and hand to the Securitate; those who hoped to attend some scientific meeting abroad could as well kiss it good-bye, not to mention the rap for those who were members of the party.

Retaliation came sooner than he thought, because— hard luck—the party secretary had his office right down the corridor. Two bullies who worked downstairs at the mechanic shop burst with the party boss into the room. They fell on him and tried to tie his hands behind his back with wire, but he slipped out of their hold, climbed on a table, flung the large window open, and threatened to jump unless they took their hands off him. The party secretary was yelling his head out, calling him a "reactionary" and threatening to have him rot in jail.

The thugs finally seized him by the arms and, punching him beneath the ribs, dragged him into a basement room in which they kept placards and posters and other public demonstration paraphernalia. They closed the door behind them carefully and were about to thrash him badly, knowing that no one from that godforsaken place would hear him cry. Rushing on him, one of them stepped on a poster that was lying on the floor. He presently started to shout he would report him for trampling under feet the shining secretary general's face. They backed off somewhat frightened, looked at each other and decided to leave him alone. "These wackos, you never know what they can do to you. Let's call a doctor to give him a shot." They locked him up in the placard room and left him there until the ambulance arrived. When the party secretary came in with the paramedics, they found him with a rusty nail in hand scribbling intricate equations on the door and patiently explaining them to a dozen big posters of the secretary general he had placed standing on their poles, along the walls. The ambulance fellows grabbed him in a jiff. One of them deftly thrust a syringe needle through the coat into his arm and soon his mind was nothing but a blur.

He woke up in a tall room with barred windows. A few chaps nearly naked surrounded him making faces and muttering indistinctly. They knocked him down and started pulling off his clothes, while a short one kept hopping around on a broomstick, laughing incessantly and neighing. Thank God a medic came in and chased them off, then picked him from the floor and dragged him out, cursing and threatening to put him back in there if he did not behave or take his medication. The burly man warned him against playing any tricks, such as slipping the pills under his tongue and spitting them out, because he'd catch him anyway and break his bones, since he had great experience breaking wise guys of his kind who did not mind their businesses and upset the party.

* * *

He was still dizzy from his fall on the stairs and now he was thirsty, too. Just a few slugs of water would have been great, but there was no water. All the utilities had been cut off. Actually, water supply had been the first to go. Last time he'd been to Tower B, people were fetching pails of water from outside to pour into the toilets. He should have bought at least a can of juice or something from the bus station store.

The black tomcat, which had continued to escort him inseparably, mewing along the corridors, was overjoyed to follow him into the chairman's office, as the place swarmed with mice. A regular hunt kicked off, with the cat searching every corner and every pile of papers on the floor.

To him, catching mice was a disgusting sight. It nauseated him, so he tried to ignore the massacre and once more slipped into the chairman's shaky seat and sat there drowsing, thinking so many schemes had been concocted and decided in that room back in the old times and even in more recent ones. They may have talked about him, too, about his case. Some people may have decided on his destiny without even as little as informing him. He was quite sure the plaster on the walls had vibrated like membranes do in microphones and that it should therefore be possible to reconstruct the voices that had planned the researchers' lives for decades. The energy, which sound waves had generated, must in some other form have been preserved in those walls that surrounded him. He began thinking of a way to extract back the voices from the walls. He started with a simple experiment. He made himself a paper funnel, put the small hole into his ear, pressed the wide mouth against the wall, and listened. He thought he might be hearing something besides the wind that raged outside, but the signal-to-noise ratio was indeed awful. What if he used several listening points along the wall? Overlapping he thought should dampen the wind noise, which was a random one, but amplify the wall voice. No sooner thought than done. He started making paper funnels, but shortly realized it was completely useless since he was there alone. He couldn't use more than two funnels and only at the corners where he could try to press both of them onto the walls at once.

The cat was bored with catching mice. His last few victims lay abandoned in a corner while he had cuddled purring on a pile of brochures between the glass-case cabinet and the ex-chairman's desk. He tried to enlist the cat in his experiment and make him listen too, but failed: Isaac just mewed in discontent and shook off the tiny funnels he had carefully crafted to match the fine, keen feline ears.

"What the hell is going on here?" he murmured disappointedly. "In these conditions I will never succeed in drawing out those sound waves. I must think up another way."

Isaac had meanwhile found a trick that seemed to entertain him greatly. Returning to his small victims, he gripped them by the tails and flung them up in the air, trying to catch them as they fell.

"I can see you are still interested in the classical side of physics," he said somewhat paternally. "It is a cinematic problem that you are trying to experiment, my friend. Though trite, you need to do it very accurately or else you won't succeed."

The tomcat was so absorbed in hurling up dead mice that he paid no notice to his lecture, but he went on nevertheless.

"Once you have understood the free fall of the bodies or, to be more specific, the free fall of the mice, you will be moving in the right direction. Your upbringing in a physics library must have had a good influence on you by sheer induction. I'm sure that in a future life, you'll make a good researcher, though with a penchant for mechanics I suppose. Actually, I had a feeling you would grow up like this and therefore did you the honor of naming you after the great Sir Isaac Newton."

The present Isaac couldn't care less about his famous name. He was making good progress and could by now hurl up the mice much higher than before and caught them, too, with perfect skill. He would have liked to talk to him about the laws of gravity, but something held him back. His previous lecture on the topic had gone terribly awry.

Back at the funny farm most of the inmates were gathered in the courtyard staring up: one of their fellows had climbed up a tree and would not come down. He stood there roaring "Me Tarzan" to the pitch of his voice. This seemed to make the others very happy for they were shouting merrily while throwing stones and whatever they found at him, while a few bobbed on all fours and squeaked around like monkeys. He thought it was not nice of them to act like that and climbed up on a bench to tell them so but nobody was listening. He also tried unsuccessfully to catch the attention of the climber and talk him into coming down. He shouted at him that the law of gravity was merciless and humans, for all their efforts, would always be governed by it. The man up there obviously didn't give a damn about the law of gravity, or any other for that matter. At times he funneled his hands around his mouth and uttered a long cry that made the buildings in the inner yard resound. He said his friends, the elephants, would hear his call and come trample the paramedics under their big feet.

His pleas eventually had been to no avail. The law of gravity had once again prevailed and Tarzan fell and broke a leg. The auxiliaries who took him away on a stretcher were mad at everyone and cursed like hell, so all the monkeys decamped as quickly as they could into the bushes and along the alleys. Later on, when the medics rounded them up and got them back into the wards, one of them clubbed him on the back, though he'd done nothing wrong but only tried to warn them about gravity.

It was getting dark outside. In the chairman's office the light had grown so dim that Isaac, the cat, had turned into a leaping shadow. "We can't go on like that. We need some light," he said and presently remembered he had to have a butt of a candle somewhere in his pockets that he had bartered from the beadle in his parish for a slice of bread. There was no electricity in his apartment building. He didn't mind because he knew the way, but had to light a candle anyway, to avoid stepping in the dark on stray dogs that slept all coiled up with the cold on the frayed doormats of his pet-loving neighbors that threw them bones and leftovers on every landing. He struck a match and lit the candle stub protecting it within his palms against the wind gusts that rushed in through the broken windows. The dancing shadows of his fingers seemed to excite the cat that frolicked around the room trying to seize them in his paws.

"Isaac, my friend, you're a complete fool," he admonished. "What you see is just a shadow, a projection of my fingers."

The tomcat seemed to understand and sobered up. Forgetting about the shadows, he jumped up on the desk and approached the burning candle. Glad to discover a new toy, he reached out to the flame, but instantly pulled back his paw, mewing in discontent.

"You're a regular fool, I tell you, Isaac. Now, meet the fire and keep in mind you're not supposed to play with it. Fire, you know, is a reaction that has made the subject among scientists of many a controversy. Ancient philosophers thought fire was one of the few basic elements on which the Universe relies."

The candle was still flickering within his palms and he could see the greedy flame devour the wax around the wick. It won't last long. He'd better put it out and save it. He might as well go on with his reflections in the dark. Actually, he was quite used to it. Electricity had been a problem in his neighborhood in both the earlier and the more recent times. During the latest period, blackouts began as soon as the winter had set in, mainly because the district-heating guys were cutting off supply over the bill arrears of the residents. As a result, most people in his building had made themselves a broad range of alternative heating devices frequently using nails instead of fuses. Ever so often, the main transformer fuse would melt plunging the entire neighborhood into pitch dark. He checked his pockets to make sure the matches were at hand if needed and blew off the candle. His eyes grew gradually accustomed to the darkness that didn't even seem so black after a while. A faint reddish glimmer that floated over Bucharest was seeping in through the large windows. Eyes sparkling in the dark, the cat was purring on the desk in front of him. He sort of envied Isaac's eyes. Their retina much more sensitive than the human one made him at home in the blackest of nights. He even considered asking the cat to guide him through the dark maze of corridors and stairways down to the broken basement window by which he had come in.

It was getting late. He knew he should be leaving but his head ached again and he felt dizzy when he tried to rise. He gave up and sat into the chairman's seat again. He wanted to rest a little, but a dense sequence of mishaps eventually prevented him.

First came the party activists who were in charge of a rally for disarmament and peace. They scoured every pavilion lab by lab to get everybody out. They said the district party branch had sent in an inspection and a television crew was on its way to cover the event and show the nation that they, nuclear physicists, were opposed to the armament race and advocated the peaceful use of nuclear energy. A red-cloth-covered podium had been raised in the courtyard and loudspeakers had been installed on the buildings to let everybody hear something special was taking place at the institute. No one was working anymore. They were struggling for peace—those were their orders. Groups of agitators posted in the first rows were shouting at the top of their lungs the usual fare of slogans, including "Ceausescu—Peace," "We want tractors on the meadows. / We don't want nuclear weapons," and "Our pride and our insignia: / Ceausescu and Romania."

He had been marched there forcibly and had no way to leave, as alert party cadres were guarding every "pass." He looked at the shouters, red in the face from crying, clapping their hands. Surprisingly, many of them were supposed to be serious researchers, people who minded their own businesses. He couldn't see the purpose of that clamor, particularly on that fine spring day when a rich sunlight bathed the blossoming bushes in the courtyard of the institute. Everyone seemed on the verge of hysteria, as if possessed by the fear of a bogy war, an unseen enemy. Some people near him started yelling "Down with the imperialists! / Let the planet live in peace!" and the crowd echoed eagerly. He took the opportunity of a short breather to remark loudly that he had a similar, though much better rhyming slogan to suggest: "Down with the secret police! / Let Romania live in peace!" Two fellows in beige parkas standing near him and probably assigned to keep an eye on his big mouth instantly punched him in the ribs. "Talking of the devil, prick?" one of them whispered in his ear. He got their point, but went on without lowering his voice: "Gosh, lads! Where is your atheistic education? Your bosses should have taught you devils are but a mystic figment." But they were hardly in the mood for joking. After another round of discreet punches in his stomach, his legs grew limp. As he was going to collapse, the parka guys snappily caught him by the armpits and dragged him out of the crowd. "Back away, please comrades, back away! The comrade's sick. We have to help him to the ambulance."

They got him into a car all right, but it was not an ambulance. Nor did they drive him to hospital but to a thicket by the beltway where there was not a soul within a mile around to witness the treatment they were going to apply to him. They put a rag into his mouth just in case, then kicked and punched him at ease, even as their curses propelled him into a space of endless sexual fantasy, at least as far as he could listen, since he passed out and did not come to until dusk half-dreaming he was a kid again and his mother was there washing his cheeks. Actually it was a cur that stood by him licking his swollen face on which the blood had curdled from a broken eyebrow. He struggled to his feet and staggered slowly to the road. He waved at several cars to no avail. Apparently, he was such a sight in the beam of the headlights that drivers sped by without a second thought. A merciful trucker eventually gave him a ride and, listening to his story, burst into an endless stream of profanities against the Securitate that had messed him up like that and even offered to drive him to a forensic doctor that he can take out a report.

"Man, I know a guy that doesn't shit his pants before any of these police and Securitate. Would you believe it: he even managed to court-martial a lieutenant who'd beaten the shit out of a cousin of mine, just like they did to you, on account he caught him with a bag of corn and said he'd stolen it from the collective farm, but he'd only picked what was left behind the students that were putting in a patriotic work stint at the farm. All right, everyone may get angry once in a while, deal a punch or two, but these cops are real crazy. They beat you for the sake of it, man. My cousin, this lieutenant thrashed him so viciously that he's a basket case to date."

At that point of the trucker's story, he choked and apparently spit some blood.

"Man, have they mangled you, those fucks! Let me drive you to hospital see if they can fix you up."

He was in a waiting room and the hospital people were asking about his papers. They said they couldn't take him in without an ID. Though he could hardly speak, he tried to tell them his papers were in his briefcase, back at the lab, and why don't they call the institute, talk to the officer on duty. Some cops had turned up out of nowhere and were questioning the trucker. It happened all the time, the medics said: drivers hit people on the roads, dumped them into the nearest hospital, and cleared away.

Eyes bulging like a frog's, the trucker was breathing his lungs out into a device that the cops had handed him, stopping every two seconds, and swearing he'd never ever pick any hitchhikers again. Now he would have to testify and have his blood and urine tested. It served him right for being kind and all instead of minding his own business.

He began telling them what had really happened and that the trucker was not responsible and only wanted to help, but he just couldn't muster enough strength to go on. His head ached terribly and speaking was too much for him. Finally, when the medics and cops started whispering to one another and let the trucker go, he grasped that maybe things were clearing up. They put a bandage on his head and told him it was nothing and he could go home, but he kept spitting blood and said he didn't want to go. He also went on saying the Securitate men had clobbered him and this seemed to piss off everyone, particularly the cops who finally proclaimed that nuts were off their turf and pulled out. The medics then shoved him into an ambulance and got him out of there. Fortunately, they didn't take him to the funny farm again. They drove him home, helped him out of the car outside his place, and told him to be good and never fight with hooligans again. He promised that he wouldn't and one of the medics walked with him into the building and told him to mind his steps. The neighborhood was plunged into darkness. It was past 10 p.m. The two hours of nightly TV program, during which the working people could enjoy power supply and watch the secretary general's working visits and the grandiose achievements of Socialism, were over now. The blackout hours had begun when they would cut off electricity to save it for the mills and factories, and put the working people straight to bed and keep them from roaming pointlessly at night. He fumbled in his pockets for the lighter, but it wasn't there. He must have lost it in the thicket where the parka guys had pounded the hell out of him for no reason at all: for voicing his personal opinion that the Romanians wanted to live in peace and wanted the Securitate that was gagging them to just let go.

It was dark all right, but he was in the chairman's office in Tower B, not in the entryway groping for his studio door. He felt somewhat relieved that the whole grim story of the Securitate men bashing him was just a replay in his mind—relieved, but apprehensive that other even bleaker moments of the past might come back to haunt him.

And so they did, as he suddenly found himself in the human resources office, the chief of personnel was sharing with the 'red hellhound,' a guy whose job seemed to consist of hating the researchers' guts and making their lives as miserable as he could. He had hardly walked in that the personnel boss started yelling at him:

"How did you dare? I'll sack you. Who do you think you are to flout internal regulations in this way?"

He didn't know what the man was talking about. Indeed they'd had a spat, but talked it out, and he believed the case was closed. Of course he was a black sheep, a reprobate, but he'd done nothing wrong this time, so he retorted in perplexity:

"I don't know what else you want me to do. I declared what there was to declare right when it happened and I have nothing more to say."

The head of personnel glared at him furiously from above the gold-rimmed spectacles that were sitting on the tip of his nose. Yes, he was still there behind his heavy oaken desk and still kept on the windowsill the old shoebox in which he tossed the photos of the hopeless, the doubtful, the problem researchers that could not be allowed to travel abroad. The suckers kept filling out complicated forms, in which they even wrote the size their peasant grandpas took their sandals. The chief of personnel would take them for a ride, handed them yet more forms, even asked them to fetch photos—for the passport, he'd say—which he tossed into the shoebox once they'd walked out the door, making fun with the "boys," his roommates.

He, too, had supplied photos to the box ever since the time where freshly out of university he got this job. Still he had never had a chance to see the uniforms of the border guards so far, because the party did not trust him.

The party was alert and watchful and wouldn't let him vanish and betray the cause, as others did on which trust had been wasted. The chief of personnel spake:

"Comrade—mind, I still do you the honor of calling you a 'comrade' though you don't deserve it—how did you dare to shirk work and go some place else while you were supposed to be at the institute?"

"What place do you mean?"

"I mean the, er, the drugstore."

"Oh now I see. So, what's wrong about it?"

"It's wrong, for you not only were away from work, but also, unlike your colleagues, refused to show your badge when we caught you standing on the queue during work hours."

"What do you mean by 'queue'? I don't know this concept and I stood on none. I was indeed to the drugstore along with other working people from our institute but for no other purpose than to align with the party policy of scientific nutrition. It was like taking part in any other political action, so I considered it was all right to do so during work hours."

The chief of personnel and the red hellhound exchanged hesitating glances. He understood he was on top and had nothing to fear from them, so he went on, embarking on a passionate tirade:

"I would like to assure you that I have studied the party documents in detail and have never missed a speech of the secretary general. Whatever you may think of me, I have a vast political culture. Now, please correct me if I'm wrong. Unlike in capitalism where working people are exploited and are paid nothing but wages, in Socialist society they receive repayment. Socialist repayment has a money constituent and a social one. The money constituent is handed out twice a month according to the payroll. However, there is no due date for social repayment, which occurs whenever the working people need certain things that they can live a decent life. Unfortunately, as we all know, some dysfunctions have affected public supply of late. The secretary general himself has noticed this state of things and asked that it be corrected. In my view, if Socialist society were better organized, public supply would never be disturbed. I ought to be able to buy something to eat when I'm hungry rather than stand in line and waste a valuable time that I could use to the benefit of society. But since I have to line up for food, I think it is only fair that society should cover this time that I lose, which thus becomes part of social repayment, and I am free to benefit by it any time I like, work hours included."

The red hellhound was foaming at the mouth. Thumping his desktop furiously, he cut in:

"Shut up, you miserable prick, or else! Don't you give us no lectures on scientific Socialism! You'd better come clean with it and say what speech you made out there while standing on the queue."

"I beg your pardon, I'm a humble person and I presume to make no speeches. However, since so many people were idling away their time out there, I figured I should tell them why they had to throng together waiting for food like that. But I didn't speak long, as the food van arrived and there was a stampede since they all struggled to keep their places in the line and some even started a row with the gypsies who were trying to get ahead of everybody else. Only a bunch of kids stayed on to listen to the end. I guess they really wanted to know why it all happened."

The red hellhound might once again have smashed him in the face, as he had done back then, but fortunately at that very moment he realized that it was just another nightmare. A revolution had taken place since then and young people had died so that no one should ever have to line up for food again and no one should fill any more shoeboxes with photos of researchers who were denied their right to travel.

Suddenly, the revolution seemed to be going on again. He was sitting in the chairman's office and the chairman was coming in right then. He looked awful, more potbellied than he remembered him. The door even seemed too narrow for his corpulence and he had to squeeze in askew. The fat man saw him sitting at his desk and started yelling:

"What do you think you're doing in my office? Out! Get out!"

But he did not cave in this time. He was the democratically elected leader of the revolutionaries. He rose from the black-leathered seat and uttered very distinctly:

"I'm sorry, sir, I'm granting no audiences today. Please see my office chief and enter your name on the list."

"What audience? What are you talking about, prick? What's got into you all? Democracy is getting to your head. Listen, you fuck! I am in charge of everything that moves in here until I am officially replaced."

"You no longer have any official capacity, sir," he countered courteously. "As of today, you are no longer chairman. I would suggest that you pack up your stuff, I mean what you think are your personal belongings in this office, and clear out at once."

The chairman seemed suddenly resigned.

"All right, lad, I'll do as you say, but get it into your head that our men will catch you all and shoot you like mad dogs. He reached out to the black phone, the one that used to shriek so loud, but changed his mind. Some cautious revolutionaries who searched the place for bugs had disconnected it anyway in case the terrorists, they said, might try to use it. Someone had turned up on TV and said there was a secret tunnel connecting Tower B to politburo headquarters in central Bucharest and that the terrorists were hiding out down there. He also said some Qaddafi men, some Arabs, had been caught carrying bomb-grade uranium in their bags. People were kind of scared and many revolutionaries toting civil defense guns had climbed up on the roofs to fight against the terrorists.

The chairman's rosy cheeks were pale and one could see he hadn't slept. He fumbled in a drawer and took out a few photos. He put them in a bag, then turned to the showcase cabinet and picked out a book about beekeeping. He grumbled like a bear, said that he would retire, that he was fed up anyway, and that research would go to pot after he was gone. As he was walking out the door, a group of armband-wearing youngsters stormed into the room, snatched his bag, and emptied it on the desk. They let him take but a few things and seized the rest. Then one of them took one more look at his things and delved out a popular science brochure, which seemed to contain a few trite things on nuclear fuel. "Gotcha, old terrorist," he shouted all worked up. They were about to tie his hands behind his back, egged on by a loudmouth, a former union toady who kept on brandishing a rifle above his head and shouting 'Down with Communism.' Another revolutionary, who sided with the Front, appeared inclined to leniency and said to let the old fart go since anyway the people would round them up and put them all on trial. As a democratically elected leader, he felt compelled to step in and set things straight. He told them to let the chairman be and even arranged for an institute car to drive the old man home, which got him under fire for protecting the nomenklatura.

Shortly afterward they summoned him to the former office of the party chapter on an excuse of founding the local Front branch at the institute. They said they'd heard it on TV that Front chapters had to be formed all across the country. He didn't realize until later that it was just a scheme to get him out of the chairman's office where some people were anxious to remove documents and valuables from the safe.

He didn't like the group that had collected at the ex-party office—a pack of rats, including the two that nearly thrashed him in the basement poster store back when he had refused to go and sort potatoes at the station. Outside the door they'd laid as mat a Ceausescu portrait that had been torn out of its frame. To him, it seemed quite a cheap thing to do.

"We all consider you a well-meaning person. We know that you were persecuted, er, under the dictatorship, that you are in fact a hero, a hero of our Revolution, that you were among the demonstrators at Romana Square that night, er, on the 21st— We gathered that they even arrested you that night—" He knew the guy that sucked up to him: an agitator, one of those who cried the loudest at the airport welcome actions.

"We would like to nominate you as a Front member, so that we fight together against the dictatorship," fawned another. "The tyrant and his hated wife have just been caught; they've just announced it on the radio."

Even as they were talking round the table, some other guys behind them were emptying the cabinets and cramming the party chapter papers into sacks. The action disconcerted him, for there sure was a good deal of evidence in those files. He asked what they were doing with the archive. Those were the orders, said a revolutionary: load it into sacks and move it out, so that every trace of Communism is wiped off the new office of the Front. He realized that whoever had ordered it had a much different thing in mind. They were dumping the sacks straight out the window in the street where several burly fellows hastily loaded them into an ambulance van.

"Gentlemen, who do you mean to save since you are calling yourselves a 'National Salvation Front'?" he asked as anger mounted to his throat. "Are you perchance going to save those who have messed up this country for decades? Right now you are smuggling out documents that are apt to become evidence against these people, and I will not condone it. You are a bunch of rogues, that's what you are!"

He walked out, yet not until advising them to stop acting as mutinous lackeys and trampling under foot the portrait of the man they'd worshipped so zealously for all those years, as this was not going to do the country any good.

"To the nuthouse, you terrorist!" he heard them saying behind his back as he left the room, in which the local Salvation Front was being hatched. He was mad at himself for leaving the chairman's office in the tower to get down there where every stool pigeon and turncoat in the institute seemed to have flocked.

He tried to climb back up into the tower, but was prevented. Guarding the door were other armband-wearing, gun-wielding youngsters, who didn't know him and wouldn't let him pass. Those were the orders. They said army troops were on their way there, that they were going to post snipers on the roof to defend the institute against the terrorists. But the terrorists never showed up to conquer the institute. That wasn't necessary: everything was falling into place already.

He could see he was out of the game and not a leader anymore, even though the real revolutionaries had democratically elected him; he was back on the blacklist, an outcast once again—this time perhaps for good.

* * *

Still looking for a way to get back into the tower, he found himself on a long dark hallway with the black cat mewing less and less heartily on his heels. He had no idea where this seemingly endless corridor was leading. He'd heard people whispering in the labs that there were secret tunnels under Tower B. He might have ended up in one of them.

It was a damp place; water was oozing from the ceiling and you could hear it drip in puddles all over the floor. The air in there was stuffy and hard to breathe. He had lit back his candle stub and was proceeding carefully protecting the shimmering flame within his hands. Big iron doors lined both sides of the corridor. Some were locked up but others stood ajar exhaling an offensive stench of animals rotting among the sewers. Rats turned up now and then, scuttled along the corridor, and vanished into some dark corner. Isaac the tomcat darted after them but every time they got within paw reach he stopped short, mewing in disgust. He obviously had no desire to stick his teeth or claws into their throats. He only wished to scare them out of instinct.

The rats themselves, once it was plain the cat was no kind of a threat, turned out in such big numbers that he had to watch his steps to avoid trampling on them. Isaac had lost the little appetite he had to chase them. His tail still stirred and he spat at them now and then, but he was clearly unnerved by the swarms of rodents that were flooding the corridor.

Somewhere a brass band began sounding a triumphal march that filled the catacombs. The music seemed to enliven the rats yet more and further droves of them were coming out from every corner and converged towards the source of the sounds.

Covering the march, a shrieking voice cried out:

"Attention, please! Attention! Ladies and gentlemen, this is an historic occasion. The first congress of the free rats is starting in a few minutes. Please, hurry to the conference hall!"

The announcement aroused his curiosity. He climbed up a few steps. In front of him, a door wide open led to a stately hall with rows of crimson velvet chairs beneath the sparkling crystal chandeliers. To his complete amazement, two rats with spiky moustaches stood on their hind legs like squirrels, mounting guard on each side of the entrance. A few others, who were apparently responsible for keeping order and wore distinctive beads around their necks, thoroughly checked everyone before they went in. No one entered until they sniffed him good around the ears and under the tail and asked him to present his claws. The bottleneck was slowing down the influx and a crowd had collected at the door. Some impatient rodents were climbing on top of the others to arrive quicker in the control area. Rows flared, with rats squeaking and scratching one another. Fortunately, a rat with shining grizzled fur and a striped ribbon on his tail noticed the brawl from inside and stepped in with authority. Once he'd bit and clawed the muzzles of a few troublemakers, order was instantly restored and everyone quietly waited for his turn.

Completely nonplussed, he had stopped in front of the entrance while the rats kept swarming in past him and nestled one by one into the crimson seats. He wondered how come he'd wound up among those disgusting animals. He'd hated rats ever since he was a kid: they killed the chicken in the coop and routed all sorts of gouges in the stables. Whenever they caught one, the villagers would smash its head and send it crushing downhill.

Was life on earth going off at a tangent? He'd never heard of rats holding congresses before. Isaac himself, frightened by those uncommon circumstances and totally reluctant to remain down there among the rats a minute longer, jumped in his arms and clutching at his coat started to whimper helplessly.

The grizzled rat had clambered on the doorjamb wherefrom he continued to watch the entrance, uttering irritated squeaks.

"Please come in, sir. Don't choke the entrance please. Even though you are human, you may join us if you like," said the same screechy voice that had announced the meeting earlier.

If anything, he was even more baffled.

"May I bring my cat along?" he asked while trying to detect the person he was speaking to.

"Of course you may. This will help demonstrate our peaceful aims and our desire to be reconciled with the feline kind."

Isaac probably missing the point of this speech had clambered up on his shoulder and was mewing in distress, while he strode over the tails of those who were still pressing in the control area and went into the conference hall.

It was not until then that he discovered the person who had addressed him: it was a rat as well, but a most venerable one wearing a little red bow on the tip of his shiny hoary tail. He was perched up on the podium clasping a mike between his forelegs and trying to stay as close as possible to the device that amplified his screech far beyond the confines of the hall, down to the remotest nooks of the galleries.

Sensing his astonishment, the red-bow rat squeaked something in his jargon, then went on in the human language:

"You shouldn't be surprised. Living side by side with the humans for so long and being used by them to various ends, some of us, most advanced rats, have learned the human tongue all right. However, since not all my fellows here can understand it, we will hold our debates in Neo-rattish squeak. As guests of honor, you will be able to hear in the headphones a simultaneous translation into human and cat speech, too, if necessary. This way, please, we have reserved these seats with headphones for our foreign guests."

"Thank you so much, but I think we really should not disturb such an important meeting," he said, while focusing on how to make the fastest exit without squelching anybody: the rat stench was suffocating him.

"No, please stay. I insist," said the polyglot rodent. "You'll see, we will have other guests besides you, as we are keen on reaching conciliation and consensus with all species. Although our people carry out their activities in barns and yards, in fields and forests, in basements, offices, and archives, we, rats, are all united around our leaders—this is the message we want to get through to our friends and foes alike."

There was no way to turn him down. He slipped into a guest seat and the tomcat sat next to him looking hugely unhappy with the tiny headphones he had to wear to understand the prattle of the hosts. The meeting was about to start when Isaac started and mewed in panic, as a stray bitch living in the sewage, another guest, sprawled in the seat beside him growling in an unfriendly way.

At last, the hoary rat opened the congress with a solemn welcome to all participants and went on to present the delegations.

"First of all, as acting president of the Free Rats Association, I wish to hail the presence in our midst of our fellows from the archives of the interior ministry, the prosecutor's office cells, the county council offices, and bank branches all around the country."

More or less cheerful squeaks emerged from the audience that started wagging their tails and thumping their paws on the backs of the seats stirring up clouds of dust.

"They are of course experienced comrades that have sniffed a great deal in their lives and on whose savvy we can rely in organizing our new society. They know how to gnaw systematically and fulfill their tasks accurately and to deadline."

The audience grew even more excited. Many rats capered and frolicked wildly in their chairs. The honorable speaker paused a minute, licked his paws in a suggestive way, fluttered the red bow on his tail, and went on:

"On behalf of our standing bureau and my own, I would also like to greet our fellows from the food warehouses, kitchens, canteens, student hostels, hospitals and drugstores, schools and kindergartens, in short— and without leaving anyone aside—all of our dedicated comrades who gnaw and gouge and make a difference wherever they live."

A frantic tail wagging, paw clapping, and exhilarated squeaking went on and on and did not calm down until the speaker's red-bowed tail tapped the lectern once or twice. The speaker himself meanwhile slurped a little water from a chipped vase and continued.

"Last but by all means not least, I wish to welcome the representatives of the rat community that lives among the miners in the pits. We will often rely on them in our future strategy. They are the best loved of us all, because the miners in their simplicity think that the rats protect their lives."

The audience burst into yet more squeaky acclaims and the delegates from the pits felt it appropriate to raise their paws with claws clutched in a show of solidarity.

Ending his greetings to the delegates, the honorable hoary rat with the red bow bid to the stand a plump, slightly balding rat that turned up from a nook carrying a hen head in his mouth. The new speaker put down his trophy, scratched his double chin, and belched before clasping the mike. He thought it fit to apologize saying he had just visited a hencoop in the neighborhood and went on.

"Most esteemed and beloved leader of our species, distinguished guests, dear friends. Many of you have known me for a long time. I've gnawed abundantly in my life ever since my apprenticeship in the royal stables when I was actually exploited by the old rats that made me steal for them oats from the horses and corn that people took to the mill for making grits. I've lived through another political turnaround in this country and—trust me—I know what it is all about. Let me tell you that any political mayhem conducted by the humans can only profit us. Back when the nationalization took place and they snatched the peasants' lands away, they gave us quite a fright. We thought they'd stamp us out, but then you know how we all thrived on the collective farms and in the deserted factories that went to seed. We found good nestling place and food galore, and our population grew stronger than ever in our history. This is precisely what will happen next. There will be troubled time. The humans will all rush into politics, while we will mind our business, as we always do. Everything will go to rot and we will have plenty to gnaw. We will have to take some measures, though. Those of you, who have been living on collective farms, forget about them, move out, and find yourselves new places in the villages, with the thrifty peasants and the former kulaks. Those who live in hospitals and schools will have no problem. Filth will grow even better and you will wallow in no end of litter. Try to make peace with the stray dogs and beggars who scrabble in the trashcans, since there will be plenty for all."

The delegates rewarded him with squeaks of pleasure and approval while the balding veteran climbed down dragging the hen head and clawing heavily to the red cloth spread over the wooden lectern.

The red-bowed honorable chairman thanked the speaker and gave the floor to a limping rodent who he said was going to present the future strategy of the organization.

"Gentlemen rodents," he began, tears welling to his eyes, "at last the day has come where we can call one another 'gentleman.' The vulgar infamous regime where we were calling one another 'comrade' is all over now. We are free rats living in a country that provides everything we need. We only have to organize ourselves. This is what I propose: Those of you, who have often sniffed and—frankly—even poked your muzzles into archive dossiers, must strengthen your positions and watch out constantly. Perhaps you do not fully realize you nestle on a heap of gold. Through your offices, we can find out anything we need to know about the species that oppose us. We'll have an edge on anyone that may stand in our way. We will be able to expose and bring down anyone we choose. The humans, prone to the vanity of grandeur as they are, will soon divide into a host of political parties and struggle against one another pointlessly. They will have no idea that the real power lies with us, rats, for we are far better organized than they are. Gentlemen, we must have some of our kin in every party's offices so we can know what's going on and, if need be, sniff every document and bank vault and any place where there is something we can gnaw at. Our rule is simple, gentlemen: We're rats, we must gnaw everything. Remember the oath you took when you first joined our organization. Whenever the humans you live with come into power and begin carving out the pie, you must make sure you send something to gnaw to your fellows starving at the opposition parties. Provided that you do so, the rodent kind will all live happily no matter who's running the country, or whether humans in this country are rich or poor. Those of you, who are planning to move into political party offices, please stay behind after the meeting that I can give you some instructions. Let's stick together! Remember our slogan: 'Rats of all countries, gnaw anything that you can get!' Long live the solidarity of rodents!"

These last words of the speaker inflamed the audience. The manifesto of the organization was unanimously approved by raise of tails.

The honorable with the red bow on his tail felt somewhat upstaged by the last speaker and the enormous thrill his message had evoked, so he, too, gave an impassionate speech to close the meeting. A weird ritual followed. Raising their tails, the rats recited in unison what seemed to be a solemn oath, but the guests could not understand a squeak, since the headphone translation had already signed off.

He had listened to every speech with quite some interest, but still found it hard to believe that the rats were so well organized. The meeting and his earlier tour of the underground galleries had tired him. His head felt heavy and he vaguely realized he would soon fall asleep.

While the rats were still squeaking their secret oath, they seemed to undergo a funny metamorphosis. Their bodies swelled and lengthened up to human proportions. Their hind leg claws disappeared into well-polished shoes and their forepaws slipped into white gloves. Their scruffy fur turned into smart tuxedos and costly fabric suits, and their heads rounded out into human faces.

He woke up in fear. Looking around, he realized the conference hall was indeed full of dignified gentlemen— no sign of tails or claws. Even the mongrel sitting right next to them turned out to be a finely dressed, hatted lady. Only Isaac and he were unchanged, ragged and dirty from rambling through the sewers with the rats.

Many gentlemen on the chairing panel looked familiar—he had seen them on TV. They made beautiful, convincing speeches to big rounds of applause. He felt confused. Perhaps he should ask someone what had happened to the rats, how come they turned into distinguished gentlemen. Finally he presumed he had been sleeping and that the rats were just a nightmare and in no way related with this fine audience.

A man in a black jacket wearing a thick gold chain around his neck and chewing gum came up to him and whispered in his ear:

"What the fuck are you doing here? How did you come in?" He said he, too, would like to know the answers to these questions.

"Look fuck, pack up your cat and beat it if you don't want no trouble!"

He obeyed, took Isaac in his arms, and went out of the hall, while he kept wondering how he'd got there in the first place. Someone must have invited him; he couldn't possibly have sneaked in through that thick bunch of guards. A few gun-wearing huskies, who were standing outside the building, didn't let him pass among the shiny limos in the parking lot. Instead they shoved him through a gangway that led him straight back into the dark corridor with water dripping from the ceiling.

3

THE SQUARE WAS PACKED AND ECHOED with vibrant down-with-Communism slogans. He was chanting heartily himself, as though those mere three words loudly repeated like a mantra would wipe away the humiliation he had suffered for so long. He'd never been so free, yet was unable to shake off a gloomy premonition.

He'd seen many former party activists around. They, too, were chanting at the top of their voices. He wondered whether he was witnessing a dramatic mass conversion or some other interests, of which opportunism was the most innocent, had brought them to that area the demonstrators were calling 'free of Communism.' There were many doubtful individuals among the demonstrators. Some were filming; others were making interviews. They pretended to be journalists, but they couldn't fool him. He knew what they were. He knew their looks and their behavior all too well. Several youngsters with the national colors on their armbands tried to check access to the square, but they were overwhelmed. There was such an outpour of intruders as though all of the gypsy women in the city could find no other place to peddle chewing gum and sunflower seeds.

The armband-wearing youngsters tried to remove them from the throng of demonstrators, but they kept coming back. They had their orders, as they said. Sometimes they even offered an apology:

"What can I do, my handsome? My turf is at the station but, you know, those guys I pay protection to says if I don't get my ass here, they see I'm never on the street again. I be damn if they don't say so. I be struck blind right here if I lie."

He was faithful to the sit-in. He would go to the square almost every day after work and stayed there until late at night. It was sort of a cleansing of the soul to him. All those who spoke from the balcony of the university building wished the country well; they wished it to be rid of Communism and bastards. He, too, spoke from the balcony one day and was acclaimed. They shouted 'Down with Communism' so loud that the whole square was rocking, but as a physicist, he realized the last word, 'Communism,' hit the walls, reverberated, and bounced back like a ping-pong ball, rolling over the demonstrators' heads like a bad omen.

It so happened that one day the coalminers were summoned from their faraway mountains to plant flowers on the square. They now lived in a democratic country and some people believed this was the right thing to do. The miners did not bring along any hoes or cuttings because they were no good at gardening; they brought clubs instead and bludgeoned anyone who walked around the place where they were ordered to plant flowers. They looked for him in his neighborhood and found him in the street, as he was coming from the greengrocer's with a bag of potatoes in his hand. A sort of commando surrounded him. There were three of them with coal smudge on their faces and miner helmets on their heads, but he knew at once they were no miners. He actually recognized them: they were some playful old 'friends' of his who had disguised as miners just to spook him. They grabbed his bag, checked his hands, and searched him for weapons. A fourth guy sitting in a Dacia car nearby took out a pile of photos from the glove compartment and poking his head out the window was leafing through them. It didn't take him long.

"Yes, he was there all right. Pinch him," he ordered. They carried him off, jabbing him in the ribs and swearing, and he did not resist—there was no way to do so. They pushed him into the back seat of the Dacia and the guy who had identified him from the snapshot drove off nervously, cursing him all the time:

"You, assholes, figured you could work it out? No way. We've had free elections. The people had their say. It's over. Knock off destabilizing the country, fucking intellectuals, dope fiends, people's fed up with you. The Americans' paying you out in dollars, ain't they, fucking bandits?"

He was driving around in circles, looking for something that he didn't seem to find. Finally, he spoke on a walkie-talkie:

"Pawn 023, checking in, sir. I've got the 'parcel,' but I can't find the 'mail van,' sir."

"Well done, 023, well done, boy!" his boss, whoever he was, said in a gratified voice. "You'll find the 'mail van' in Marasesti Square."

They turned him over to another squad that squeezed him into a packed van. Crammed together, men and women were stifling inside. Many were bruised and injured; some were bleeding. The car was bumping, squeaking at the joints, on what seemed to be a back street of some kind. He hoped it would finally break apart and set them loose, but it didn't and then the road seemed to improve as well. They had no idea where they were going. A woman screamed they were going to shoot them dead somewhere on the outskirts. He didn't think it would be possible: they did live in a democratic country after all; at least that's what they said on TV. Actually, it was in the name of democracy that they'd been rounded up: because they disagreed with a majority of overblown housewives that had acclaimed the miners as they rampaged through the 'Communism-free' square, clubbing as many destabilizing intellectuals as they could lay their hands on.

The van finally stopped at a military unit where they were dumped and forced to stand on a concrete platform framed on all sides by guys with truncheons at the ready. Then they were searched for weapons and marched, hands up behind their heads, through a welcoming corridor specially designed for them. He later found out it was called a gantlet: two rows of burly guys that looked like robots as they struck the file of prisoners with their bludgeons. They didn't swear or say anything; they just struck calmly, coldly, heavily. This was their job. They were full-grown adults; some even with gray hair, who did their job thoroughly, without any emotional involvement. Not a muscle stirred on their face. He was thrashed like everybody else, but didn't really feel the blows so much; his mind was somewhere else, in the cozy intimacy of a family where the father was coming home from work late and his child was pleased to see him. "Mom, hey, Mom, Daddy's home." And the mother, an apron on her dress, was coming out of the kitchen to say hello. He kissed her tenderly. "How was it today, darling, another hard day?" she asked, patting him on the cheek. "The usual," he said sullenly. "Have you reined in those troublemakers?" "Fucking idiots. I pounded them till my hand ached. One of them trying to shun a blow got on my nerves and I hit him even harder. I crushed his eye and the white gushed out on his chest." "Oh dear! Will these louts never stop it? Can't they see they haven't got a chance? How can they even dream we'll let them run the country that they bring back the kings and landowners to exploit the people again?"

He wondered if there was any methodology for beating demonstrators and whether work safety standards were provided, since this job had its hazards. Firstly, one had to strike from some regulated distance. Standing too close to the victim was risky, as you could be splashed with blood and get infected with some lethal virus, some incurable disease. Besides, one had to avoid striking any vital organ, or else the client passed out and it was no fun any more. You did not have the thrill of watching him smart and writhe in pain. Maiming the guy was also ill advised, as this could get you into trouble with the forensic examiners that would not miss the opportunity of squeezing some hush money from you. There had to be a code of best practice in mauling, though it was probably unwritten and was transmitted orally from one fiend to another as some sort of caste lore.

The blows had made him woozy and silly visions kept coming to his mind. He imagined one of his tormentors living to be a grandfather and sitting on the terrace of a plush villa in an exclusive neighborhood telling his grandchildren how he'd fought for the revolution as a real hero and had even a certificate to prove it. The grandchildren, however, did not seem really interested in learning exactly how all the benefits they now enjoyed had come into the family. Growing up in a villa with a shiny jeep and a swimming pool, they had no idea their grandpa had beaten, stolen, and kowtowed to provide them with their current wealth. He was a kind old chap, exchanging greetings with the neighbors and teaching healthy moral principles to his grandchildren who never even heard his words, let alone heeded them. There is this youngest grandson, though, this little brat rattling all day a toy machinegun with many colored lamps. This one would pester him with embarrassing questions.

"Say, Granddaddy, how many people did you shoot in the revolution?"

"I didn't shoot no one, teddy bear. Where do you get such things into your little head? The dictator ordered fire against the demonstrators and the army opened fire."

"It did not. It was you. I am the Master Spy and I know everything. I know it was you. I heard you say so."

"What is it that you heard, teddy bear?"

The grandson rattled his gun and his question again:

"Tell me, Granddaddy! Ten? Did you kill ten?"

"What did you hear me say?"

"I heard you talking with your friend Jenica. You were dead drunk and thought nobody listened, but Master Spy was there." And the little urchin banged his gun again at his granddaddy shouting merrily: "You're dead, Granddaddy! Master Spy has got you. Master Spy has killed you."

They took him upstairs to take his fingerprints and question him. There were two plainclothesmen sitting at a table and a military that was typing at a smaller table. They asked him stupid, biased questions but he clammed up and answered none of them. Perhaps he would have answered if only his mind hadn't been so distracted right then.

"Grandpa, our history teacher is telling us the coalminers' raid back in the 1990s was a retrograde incident that scared away foreign investors and isolated our country from Europe for a long while. He says it was an attempt by the Neo-communist authorities to suppress political opposition."

"He lies. It was not at all like that."

"But he says plenty of evidence has turned up that they were not all miners, that most of them were former Securitate men."

"Bullshit! Big fat lies, that's what he's telling you."

"But is it true you clubbed many intellectuals and incited the workers against them?"

"Not really. Some intellectuals got caught in the turmoil, but it was all their fault, because they didn't mind their own business and liked to meddle in everything. Besides, they didn't recognize the legitimacy of the first free elections."

"Our teacher says those elections were rigged. He says the peasants had been deliberately frightened that the landowners would come and seize their lands and the workers had been told foreign capitalists would take their factories and turn them jobless, and that they were all so deeply brainwashed that they were marching in the streets chanting, 'Ourselves we do not think, we work'."

"He tells you packs of lies, this teacher. I'll speak to the people at the ministry to have him transferred to some smaller school."

"But he's cool, Grandpa, and we like him. Anyway, drop this. Tell me how many intellectuals did you beat back then during the miners raid?"

"I didn't beat no intellectuals. I beat hooligans. They were all hooligans. Instead of going to work, they were hanging out in the streets, shouting about democracy and freedom, and even had the guts to stand up against us when our people were trying to restore order and quiet."

"Yeah, I know, I know, that's what you called the intellectuals: 'hooligans.' How does it feel to beat someone, Grandpa? Someone that can't defend himself?"

"Look, grandson. Stop bothering me with all this rubbish. If I hadn't beaten those guys and many others, too, you'd have got nothing of all you have today. You wouldn't drive yourself to school and would get thrashed by gypsies on the streetcars. You wouldn't live in this great villa, but in a cheap tenth floor apartment in the housing projects, and instead of swimming in your pool, you would be bathing in the shitty swamps on the outskirts. I have struggled to provide all this. If we hadn't seized power back then, others would have done so and would have acted exactly as we did. But we were better organized than anyone and we succeeded. And that's how you have everything you like, while other kids your age don't have shit, even though they may be smarter than you are. So don't you try lecture me and let me lecture you instead, because it's time you learn how one has to seize power and not let anyone stand in his way, smash them, shoot them, if necessary, because there is no law except one: it is the stronger guy that wins and the stronger guy is the one who's loaded."

He had no idea whether the grandsons of tomorrow would like what their grandfathers would answer them. Anyway, time would go by and things would be forgotten; the history textbooks would here and there be doctored, watered down.

Evil is easily forgotten when ignored. It was exactly what he was trying to do with the plainclothesman that was questioning him—ignore him—even though the guy was raging by now, swearing at him, calling him a 'destabilizer,' and smacking him like mad. He kept poking photos under his nose, snapshots they'd made down at the University Square, asking him to identify those faces, but he didn't breathe a word. He didn't even say he didn't know those people. He had nothing to say.

"Take this jerk away or I'll throw him out the window," the detective eventually gave up. They dragged him by the arms into a corner, near an iron barred window that overlooked the inner yard.

Down there, some guys donning miners' outfits were getting off a bus. They took off their overalls and helmets, handed them to a non-com along with their miners' lanterns, and went to wash their faces at the water pump. A row of acacias lined the view in the distance. Through a gap in the leafage, he suddenly caught the familiar glimpse shimmering in the summer heat of the metallic atom and of the selfsame Tower B beneath it. It finally dawned on him where he was. He'd passed by this military unit many times when they were going out to sort potatoes. It was on the road to the station and he knew it was a Securitate unit. He'd never figured it would become a miners' place as well.

Those were troubled times. The stronger strangled the weaker in the name of democracy. Of all that was happening to him, he could realize he was going in the wrong direction, and that the purpose of his life was elsewhere. He was a researcher and should concern himself about research, but the conditions to do so were growing harder and harder, and the institute itself was going down as if on a slide.

All this was helter-skelter coming to his mind. He couldn't realize whether those were just recollections, or he was living it all up again. He was convinced that everything in both history and life was moving in circles

Tired and numb, he was crouching in a corner of the chairman's office. It was a stormy night outside. The wind was wailing and the ravenous dogs were howling wild around the tower. The tomcat cuddled by his hip and purred, and he remembered the shepherds that had given him shelter in the desert. He tucked his coat closer around him and rested his head onto his arm. He didn't want to sleep; he was simply trying to go back and find the road to Nineveh, as he was ordered. He'd lost his way in the dark and felt sorry for not taking the hide of water the shepherds had offered him. He'd never been so thirsty in his life.

*   *   *

The path wound down among dry shrubs into a narrow vale that was protecting a patch of green against the parching sun. His scorched lips ached for a few drops of water. He would have liked to be the cricket or the lizard that he had bid to drink. He'd noticed from the ridge the sparse green tufts strewn at the bottom of the valley and hurried down, hoping that there would be some water too, but there was none. All that the drought had spared was a small bog with a few frogs that leapt for cover as he showed up. He had neglected the shepherds' offering, but was somehow confident he would not die of thirst. The sun glared mercilessly and he felt as if a fireball was melting up above him, raining hot flows of lava on his shoulders, making him totter weakly, yet he hoped he would soon come in sight of Nineveh or meet a caravan or other charitable shepherds that would give him rescue.

He trudged and left the muddy vale behind and, having lost his path again, halted and looked around him. He knew there had to be a merchants' road out there leading to the great city. His heart throbbed full of gratitude and hope as a human silhouette and a few donkeys with burdens on their backs showed up beyond the reddish rocks. "It is perhaps a merchant going to Nineveh. The journey will seem shorter if we could keep each other company."

He cut across the shriveled shrubs and rugged stones and reached the road. Much to his surprise, it was a woman that drove the donkeys. Her head was wrapped up in a long black scarf that covered her body like a cloak down to her knees. Her barren feet were hurt and bleeding from a long walk across the craggy, thorny wilderness. She was walking apace and startled to see him turning up so suddenly before her. She stopped and cried out brandishing her iron-pommeled staff:

"Stay out of my way, stranger! Do me no harm, or else my kinsmen will catch up with you. They will destroy you and scatter your ashes to the four winds."

"Don't think ill of me, daughter of the Earth, conceived from pleasure and cast into the world to earn your bread in pain," he said and kneeled, humbly bending his head in front of her. "I am neither a malefactor nor a robber. You have nothing to fear. I'm only begging you to tell me where I can quench my thirst with a few drops of water."

The woman looked at him bewildered.

"Stand up, stranger! Don't let your knees lie in the dust before a woman! I've never seen nor heard of anyone among my kin behave like that. If you're so thirsty as you say you are, follow me and you'll find a clear, cool spring not far from here where the mountains rise from the ground and the valley snakes through the rocks. I'm heading there myself to fill these hides."

He stepped out of the path and let her go ahead.

"I'll let you guide me, daughter of the Earth. Take us both swiftly to that clear cool spring you spoke about."

She moved ahead leading the way, followed by her three donkeys carrying empty hides, while he, head low, brought up the rear. Humbling his mind and wearying his body he thought would help him see his journey to an end.

Ahead of him, the woman walked proudly on, as one who was in her familiar surroundings, and seemed to take no more notice of him than she took of her donkeys. She didn't ask him anything and he said nothing, yet she remembered him every once in a while, as she urged on the donkeys, and cheered him up:

"Hang on! We'll be there presently."

They had been walking up the valley a long way when he thought he could hear a murmur coming from the ground. They were above the wellspring, said the woman. Soon enough they were to find the spring.

As they came in sight of the place where water gushed out from the bowels of the earth through greenish stones, the donkeys rushed to drink and the woman said with a cunning smile:

"Go ahead, stranger, quench your thirst and, when you're done, repay your guide that led you to this place and fill those hides on the donkey's backs. I'll go and cleanse my body meanwhile in the pond downstream. There has been a new moon…"

He cast at her a glimpse of understanding:

"All right! Go wash your body of impurity. I'll fill the hides and bind them on the donkeys' backs, as you have ordered."

She once again smiled slyly and bent down to drink from the same puddle where the donkeys had appeased their thirst.

"Drink, stranger! I thought you said you're dying for a gulp of water, now you're shying away—"

"I will drink, but not until I thank the Lord, my God, who made the Heavens and the Earth, and ordered clear springs to pour out of the rock and slake our thirst." And as he said so, he raised his arms toward the sky and stood so without moving. The woman looked at him, amazed by his uncommon conduct. She then searched in her bags, took out a pitcher she used for filling up the hides, put it down at his feet, and hurried eagerly toward the pond.

Once he was done with praying, he washed his hands and face at the spring, let the clear water flow in his rounded palms, and drank. Sated, he started filling up one by one the hides and fastening them on the donkeys' backs, as the woman had asked him to do in return for her guidance.

From beyond the shrubbery, he heard the water splashing as the woman bathed. He prayed in his heart to drive away any temptation and, once his chore completed, sat on a boulder by the spring. He would have liked to call the donkeys' mistress in some way, tell her he had fulfilled his task, and be off. He even thought of walking there backwards in order not to see her nakedness, but had no time to make up his mind, as the woman's wet hands clasped his shoulders and her dripping hair shrouded his face.

"Good fortune brought you my way, stranger," she said. "I've cleansed myself of the uncleanness I have every new moon and I now wish to privilege you with my body—"

He winced and felt suddenly breathless:

"Away with you, temptation! Do not defile my body and spirit!" he cried and drew aside in fear.

The woman was naked and water was dripping from her hair. Thinking she was a vision, one of the evil spirits that tortured him at night, he turned his eyes away and murmured in disgust:

"Begone! A curse on you forever!"

The woman burst into roaring laughter then found a smooth place on a rock and laid her naked body in the sun, closing her eyes and saying:

"Let this man give me a son and the wish of my people be fulfilled this way! Let his manhood awaken and let him not drive me away, nor falter as he lies with me!"

"Stop talking like this, woman!" he scolded her raising his staff as if to drive her off. "Go lie with whom you've lain before, go after men of your own people, and don't try to defile me, or tempt me with your nakedness. Put on your clothes, take your donkeys, and be off. I've filled the hides for you, as you requested. Don't make me cast a curse on you for troubling my spirit."

"Don't punish me, stranger! Don't drive me off your sight!" she said getting down on her knees. "Be merciful and suffer that I enlighten you on why I beg your manhood and want to lie with you."

"Put on your clothes first and I'll listen," he said trying hard to keep his eyes away off her ripe breasts that showed among the tresses falling loosely on her shoulders. Then, as the woman did not seem to have any intention to cover up her nakedness, he turned his face off her and went on saying:

"Don't you have enough men around you in your people? Isn't there anyone among them capable to sate your lust? Why, of all men, will you tempt me? Have I wronged you in any way?"

The woman buried her face in her hands and started weeping in distress. Still puzzled and fighting off the temptation that kept nagging him, he turned, put his hands on her shoulders, and raised her from the ground:

"Why are you weeping, daughter of the Earth? Is your lust so great or are there other reasons that make you kneel before me and beseech my manhood?"

Sighing and wiping off her tears, she answered:

"Bless you, stranger, and may you walk the path of righteousness forever! Please bear with me and suffer that I tell you about the plight of my poor people that toil leading their flocks along this valley. Neither I nor any other woman of my people capable of bearing sons can have any. A curse is on us and a scourge has visited our land. A ball of fire fell from the sky and dug a huge hole in the ground not far from our village. Our men went there and searched the place looking for a treasure or other valuable things. But they had hardly touched the fallen rock that they were struck with impotence and barrenness. Our people is dying out. We, women, therefore, as we meet strangers, fall on our knees before them and beseech them to give us sons."

He listened to her story with sympathy, but would not even glance at her. His hands were now grasping her thighs yet he appeared not more excited than if he'd held an ewer. Nothing in his appearance seemed to reveal the natural desire that any man would feel touching the warm young body of a woman.

"A dreadful curse indeed has struck your people," he nodded sadly. "The angels of the Lord fly all around the Earth and keep the fireballs from falling down and wreaking harm. When they do fall and crash against the face of Earth, it is because the guardian angels let them through to punish us because we dwell in sin. Listen to me and tell your people to stay away of that the fireball, for everything around is poisoned and will remain so for a long time. Leave your village and move out of there and don't let your animals graze anywhere near that place, because the males of your flocks and herds that do so will also become barren and your livestock will decline as your people will. Go down the valley and look out for the Moabites. You, young and fertile women lie with their men and bear them children. The men of Moab are well known for their strength and vigor and where they spread their seed peoples have grown in numbers and filled the land."

"My people and Moab are enemies because our forefathers and theirs fought against one another and shed one another's blood. Should our men find out we lie with Moabites, they would stone us to death, as they did to those of us that went to Nineveh and, instead of returning with offspring in their wombs, whored with the Ninevites who spilled their seed away and did not give them sons."

"I understand your anguish, daughter of the Earth. If it is the desire to increase your people rather than lust that has been driving you in search of men, may this desire of yours be soon fulfilled. As for me, I have other things to do. I am not to lie with alien women, nor indulge in the pleasures of the flesh, as I have other orders to accomplish."

Upon these words, the woman aroused and throbbing to feel his hands on her thighs burst desperately into tears.

"Don't drive me away, master, nor withhold from me the fire of your body. In this wilderness it may be a long time until I run across another man."

He didn't listen to her any longer. He took his hands off her, washed himself in the coolness of the spring, then picked up his staff and went away without looking back. He could hear her sobbing behind him by the spring while he walked hurriedly praying that temptation should not have the best of him. Squeaky voices were calling him from the green shrubbery around the pond, teasing him, urging him to go back to the hot body aching with desire of the woman. He was not ready to fall for such tricks. He was anxious to get to Nineveh because the tablets with the ancient writs were in great danger. Temptation walked ahead of him and behind him, to his right and left, and would not let go of him, but he had to hold his own, otherwise he would not be able to save the ancient writs in which the science and wisdom of the peoples lay. The voice had ordered him to do so in the wilderness and he was going to obey.

The satchel seemed to be hanging in the shrubs on purpose, as though to catch the eye of the first passer-by. He had noticed it from a distance and thought at first it might belong to some traveler that would have stopped there for a rest. But there was no one. Seen from the top of the valley, the road winding between the rocks seemed desert, too. He reached out for it reluctantly, as one would do for someone else's good, and freed the strap from the thorns that kept it tangled. He thought he might find food inside, perhaps even a flask of water. It wasn't meant to be this way. The satchel was stuffed with rags in which a pure gold goblet studded with emeralds was wrapped. He couldn't believe his eyes and how could he since its sparkle almost bedazzled him. Suddenly, a laughter very similar to a neigh burst forth and fawning voices congratulated him and told him he was rich: he'd come across a treasure-trove that would make him the master of many flocks and slaves, and rank him with the proud and wealthy.

He scolded the voices and did away with the temptation presently, hurling the goblet as far as he could into the gully and keeping just the leather satchel that suited well the wayfarer he was, determined to cut across the wilderness to execute his order.

Kicking a stone, the goblet rang like a bell and the sound lingered in his ears as a reproach urging him to go back and find the precious vessel and take it with him. He hurried on and never looked back while everything was getting mixed up in his mind and he began to wonder whether the naked body of the woman by the spring and the gold goblet were anything but figments of the spirits trying to make him stumble on his way and lead him astray. The night was falling but he had no intention to stop. He feared the woman that had offered him her body, or the owner of the valuable goblet that had hung the satchel in the bushes might catch up with him.

It was dark already and he still groped along the path, with craggy stones ripping his feet. He wanted to keep going. He thought he glimpsed the lights of Nineveh twinkling against the nightly sky. Only much later, as the moon rose shining from among the clouds, he saw that he was wrong—the city wasn't where he thought she'd be. As he slowed down decided to find a shelter on the roadside, he saw a bonfire in a little vale and headed that way. "If those are honest merchants driving their caravans, I have nothing to fear; and if they're brigands of the wilderness, there's nothing they can take away from me."

Despite this reasoning, he approached the fire somewhat stealthily and found a group of merchants had stopped their caravan there for the night. Camels and donkeys were lying down, while a few servants were gathering dry brushwood to keep the fire alive till dawn.

Another servant was kneading dough to make bread. Smelling the stranger, the dogs started to bark while a guard sitting by the bags drew his sword and came his way asking sternly from some distance:

"Who are you? What do you want?"

"I'm just a weary traveler as you are," he answered and, since the dogs were surrounding him baring their fangs, he kneeled down on the road and lowered his head nearly to the ground. The dogs uncannily stood still and the guard, too, stopped in amazement:

"Stand up, stranger, and come with me. I will present you to my master, as no one cannot be allowed to join our camp without his approval."

He rose to his feet and, followed by the guard, walked to the fire where the servants glanced at him suspiciously:

"Aren't you one of those robbers of the wilderness coming to spy on our camp?" one of them questioned him.

"I am no robber, brothers, and the Lord knows that I have done no wrong to anyone."

"How's that 'no wrong,' you good-for-nothing scoundrel?" said another pointing to the satchel he carried on his shoulder. "This is our master's food bag that was stolen from us as we stopped over in a cedar valley yesterday. How dare you turn up at our camp flashing the very good you stole from us?"

The other servants, too, halting whatever they were doing, gathered around him, drawing their blades as though everyone was determined to cut out a piece of him.

"Calm down, brothers!" he said as kindly as he could. "Don't let rash impulse cloud your minds. Don't take my life until you know for sure I was the robber. I found this satchel hanging in the shrubs along the path."

"He's lying," cried out a servant.

"Let's kill him!" said another.

"We'd better torture him first," joined in a third one with a salt-and-pepper beard that seemed to be their boss. Let's put him on the rack, make him confess his crimes, and when the master climbs down from the mountain, he'll try the villain and punish him as meet."

"Where is your master now?" he ventured to ask.

"He's gone up the mountain to read the stars and find out what is going to happen," said the bearded man. "Our master is a wise man and won't waste any time listening to your phony gabble."

"Being a wise man, I presume he'll listen. And I'll tell him what I found in this bag in which you said there had been food when it was stolen from him."

"I say we'd better keep the rules," cut in the guard that had taken him to the fire. "The master will try him and we will carry out the sentence as usual and smash his head against the stones."

And saying so, he tied his hands with a thick rope and fastened the other end around the neck of a camel that was lying by the fire.

"When do you think your master will be back to try me?" he asked candidly.

"Don't rush to punishment. Your end is near anyway," said the chief servant grinning, as he poured himself a horn of wine.

"Our master will be down after midnight, as usual," said the guard that had bound him up. "Watch your tongue by then, say nothing inappropriate to anyone, and don't take it into your head that you can run away."

Hands tied behind his back, he sat down near the camel and raised his eyes to the starry sky, paying no further notice to the servants that sipped their wine around the fire where the bread was baking filling the air with a sweet fragrance. They laughed and called him names and teased him on how they'll torture him to death, but he was too tired to care. He lay down on the ground and soon was fast asleep.

* * *

He was in the revolution again. Riot police had turned him over to a plainclothesman that was cursing him and kicking him haphazardly wherever he could get. He was handcuffed and on his knees along with others on the sidewalk, while a Securitate serviceman pointed a submachine gun at them. "Private, if anyone moves: shoot him! You get that?" the plainclothesman would order him every few minutes. "Yes, Com'd 'tenant!" the man said as an automaton, yelling to make himself heard over the uproar. Machineguns barked like bitches from the armored cars, spitting their fire along the avenue. Shells sprinkled all around like fireworks. At times, as their rattle stopped, the chorused slogan of the crowd rose from behind the barricade: "Free-dom! Free-dom! Free-dom!" The buildings echoed the voices of the hopeless protesters toward the firing line, enraging the plainclothes agents clad in typical leather jackets, who paced furiously among the military, yelling like mad and sometimes even wrenched the guns from their hands to show them how they were supposed to shoot.

"Carry out the order! D'you hear me? Fire! What the hell! You'll all wind up in court martial!"

From where he was standing on his knees he could see tracers darting from the barrels and putting light streaks in the sky, but not much else. One of the plainclothesmen, who was holding a gun in his hand, appeared to be the boss. He was moving imperatively to and fro, asking everyone to listen to his order and fire on a car from behind which a group of youths were chanting impudently in their direction: "Mur-de-rers! Mur-de-rers!"

Everything was upside down and the uniformed officers somehow seemed to have no power. The plainclothesmen in leather jackets wielding radiotelephones and guns had taken over. A car pulled up in a shrill sound of brakes a few meters away, framing him and the other prisoners in the glare of the headlights. It was his first chance to discover who the other kneelers were: kids mostly, with bold faces, tousled hair, and torn clothes. The guy, who got off, waddled like a duck. All he could see of him were his army boots and the hem of his leather coat gleaming in the lights of the car.

The troops were ordered to hold fire. The waddling guy must have been some big shot, he gathered, since one of the plainclothesman came up to brief him. He didn't like what was going on, particularly as some of the pert youths kneeling out there suddenly burst up chanting, "Down with the dic-ta-tor! Down with the dic-ta-tor!" And all the kneelers presently chimed in. He was shouting his lungs off himself and was surprised to learn he had the guts to do so. He was glad to be there down on his knees, yet not defeated, alongside those cheeky kids that nothing frightened any longer.

"Who do you think you bunch of traitors want to overturn?" yelled the big boss bounding among them as a polecat among the chicken. He kicked and pummeled sweepingly, and went on swearing. "D'you have anyone better than he, fucking reactionaries?"

He, too, got a boot in the back and, as he turned to see who'd done it, he caught a glimpse of the man's face and recognized him. The waddler was not just another nameless apparatchik, but a big wig of the party. The thought flashed through his mind it was some kind of a privilege to be kicked by a high Communist official and he was not sorry at all for being there where the fate of the Romanians was decided.

As he'd arrived at work in the morning, nothing seemed to foretell what was going to happen. The party activists looked more in control than ever, touring the labs, testing the mood, supplying the 'correct' version of the latest developments. The secretary general, they said, had been right. In Timisoara, the hooligans had attacked military units and this was why the soldiers had fired.

Then the order came out the institute employees were to go to the rally. Not all of them: party members only. He stayed behind in the lab, all fidgety, trying to work his anger off. He was furious against himself for turning into a coward. People were dying for freedom in Timisoara, even as he stood there, doing nothing, having the jitters. Why had he listened to Free Europe at all? He kept hearing again and again those desperate cries of the demonstrators, the rattle of the guns, and felt as powerless as a worm.

When his first workmates came back from the city scared, with muddy, crumpled clothes, and no posters or banners, he realized something was happening: the end had just begun. One of the institute buses had drawn up outside Tower B and a cadre was rebuking the driver for failing to collect the banners the party members had abandoned in their flight. The driver muttered it was not his business; he kept trying to put back into the frame a poster of the secretary general sporting a brand new Fuehrer moustache added by some brazen reactionaries. Looking at it, the activist got frightened and told the driver he'd better hide "that one" as soon as possible, just leave it: many others were missing anyway and they would have to report them lost.

"Gentlemen, stop this nonsense, will you? It's over anyway," he said.

Humbled, the activist did not react as usual—calling him a reactionary and so on—but just lowered his eyes pretending to care about the shreds of banners scattered in the bus: yes, he was scared.

This buoyed him up. He jumped into the first car riding to the city. He made several attempts to reach the epicenter of the revolt, but couldn't make it. The cops and riot police had set up roadblocks not only at the ends of the main avenue but also on the smaller streets leading to it. He could hear the demonstrators shouting—a rumble floated in the air and flowed among the buildings spreading the hope for freedom. Once again he felt a coward for not being at the heart of the revolt where others he had so often branded chicken in the past were boldly claiming their rights—and his. The night was falling gloomily. Death arrows ripped the sky: they were firing tracers somewhere around Romana Square. Meanwhile, the cordon near him gave in and a few youths ran by with riot police on their heels.

"Hey, let them be. What have they done to you?" he cried feeling he had to take a stand. It was all they needed. The plainclothesman that was in command of the riot cops snapped, "Grab this one too," which they readily did, adding a few truncheons on his back as a foretaste, but he didn't feel any pain; he was happy: something was happening at last in his country as well. He even felt like he ought to thank those cops that marched him like an animal, swearing and pounding him all over to make him move faster. They were taking him precisely where he wanted to be.

He was waiting for the party big shot to cool down and stop kicking and pummeling. He thought he would have a chance to talk with the others, ask them why they had taken to the streets, but no way. The party man was frantically striking everyone around. When one of the kneelers, a teenager, shouted, "Murderer," at him, he went berserk and started kicking the youth in the head, tearing his face apart. But the kid was stubborn and went on yelling as loud as he could though he was spitting blood already.

He couldn't see who fired that bullet. He only saw the kid's head burst and his brain spurting out in blobs mixed up with blood. He couldn't believe this was happening. All that crap about Socialist humanitarianism and everything was going down the drain; the party was at war and resolute to stay in power at all costs.

"I'm gonna shoot you all, fucking reactionaries!" the big shot roared and then he realized who had blown up the kid's brain. He might have done it to set an example to the rank and file, who preferred to not adjust their fire and let their bullets bite at trees and buildings.

He felt he had to do something, but could come up with nothing clever. He wanted to taunt the big shot, say something to make him stagger. A quote from the secretary general perhaps. It usually worked, but not this time. The time of words was over. They were shooting people down there.

A plainclothes agent came up with a radiotelephone in one hand and dragging with the other a sort of lump that turned out to be an old peasant woman clutching a ragged bag and crying out loud. While he was pulling her by her hair before the big boss as some kind of trophy, the woman, who was already scared to death, noticed the kid lying in a puddle of blood and started crying even louder, begging them not to shoot her. She was just a countrywoman, she said. She didn't know what was going on there and had only come to Bucharest to fetch some dry plums to make compote for her little grandson. They had seized her by mistake, she kept saying. Then, as if to make her case, she stooped and fumbled in her bag and took out a handful of plums to show them, but the man who'd dragged her over cursed her and kicked her in the hand making the fruits fly off and roll into the puddle of blood among the splinters of the dead kid's skull. He realized the plums were mingled with clods of brain and they all looked alike as they lay scattered on the pavement, and felt like he was going to throw up.

"What am I to do with her, comrade minister? Shall I shoot her?" asked the moron who'd brought her over and took out a gun from his belt. He probably meant to show his boss that he, too, although an underling, was just as resolute and brave and ready to shoot anyone without scruples or mercy when the cause of Socialism and Communism was at stake.

"Go ahead, shoot the fucking old bitch," the comrade minister answered with an uncertain drawl and a nauseated look on his face as he stared at the woman's plums scattered in the bloody muck. He seemed nervous; something was bugging him; he was sorry perhaps that he had pulled the trigger in front of everybody, shooting that wretch that had dared defy him.

He felt he ought to do something. The gray haired woman crawling on the ground, begging for mercy looked like his mother who he knew was far away in her remote village lost in the hills. Perhaps it was she all right, coming to fetch him some dry plums, knowing there was almost no food available in Bucharest.

"She's my mother. Don't you shoot my mother!" he cried out in despair. "She's done nothing wrong. She just came to fetch me some plums."

The minister turned to him baffled that a reactionary under arrest had the nerve to intervene and talk to him asking for mercy.

"And who the fuck are you that you dare speak to me?"

He felt bold enough to confront him and uttered quite distinctly:

"Sir, I apologize for not being able to call you 'comrade' but I have no comradeship with killers. I will personally inform the secretary general of the murder you have committed in front of everyone here so that he may realize the kind of people he relies on. In your capacity as a minister you should try to appease the situation instead of destabilizing it further and wreaking havoc."

He would have had more to say but a ministerial boot in his stomach promptly silenced him.

"Listen to this! A reactionary's telling me what I must or mustn't do!" he shouted angrily.

No one on the armored carriers was firing any more. They were waiting for orders. The lull emboldened the demonstrators behind the barricade, who started chanting, "Free-dom! Free-dom!" waving national flags, from which they had ripped off the Communist emblem. In the meantime, more and more protesters were being caught and marched to where he continued to stand on his knees.

"In the vans. Put all of them into the vans. Arrest them all reactionary motherfuckers," yelled the minister." It was no doubt a major change in tactics. He was not ordering any more shooting, just arrests. Perhaps he'd been well inspired saying what he'd just said. Many lives were perhaps saved as a result.

To get to the vans, they had to walk between two rows of riot cops who thought it fit, just in case their commanders were looking, to show some zeal and didn't spare their blows. He got away with a cracked rib and a few big bumps on the head. He could have ended up much worse but for a stern voice that made them restrain their impulses: "Enough, let him go. We want him alive. Looks like he is their boss. We'll make him squeal."

The van filled up rapidly and they had to squeeze the last ones in. A woman cried that they'd broken her arm. A young man with a blasted eye said he could see no more and was asking someone give him a handkerchief to staunch the bleeding. He tried to reach at the hankie he knew was in the pocket of his anorak, but couldn't make it. The handcuffs hurt his wrists behind his back and he had no way to move his hands except a little bit.

They got off at Jilava prison.

"Welcome!" the cops shouted and started to freshen them up with their truncheons. Then they were crammed men and women together into a cell for selection. A pregnant woman said her pains had started. They'd kicked her in the belly, she said. The young man with a blasted eye was shouting that he be taken to a doctor, but a seasoned guard, who seemed to know what lay in store for them, told him with a grin:

"What d'you need a doctor for? They'll shoot you in the morning anyway."

After some time, those who were seriously wounded were taken somewhere else. The lad whose eye was hurt was clinging to him. He looked like he was going nuts, as he kept saying, "I don't want to die, uncle. I'm young, uncle. I want to live, not die!"

Between hope and fear, the night was slow to pass away. They were too many in the cell to be able to sleep. Someone suggested they should sing, "Wake up, Romanian," and so they did filling the prison corridors with their voices.

"Knock it off, assholes!" the guards yelled. "Knock it off, or else we turn on the heat on you!"

A young boy had climbed up close to the ceiling where the barred window was and told them what was going on in the yard outside. He let them know when yet another van with prisoners was coming in. And they kept coming. At one point in the wee hours, they could hear metal barrels being unloaded from a truck outside and someone in the cell said they'd probably brought in sulfuric acid from a factory not far from there. "They'll pour it on our bodies after they shoot us in the ditch," he said.

In the morning the prison turned eerily silent. The guards looked pale and had turned very kind all at once. They would come ask around if anybody needed anything. After a while, they took the prisoners out of the cell and led them into the yard. Instead of the death squad, buses were waiting. They told them they'd been forgiven just for once, but that they should be careful, for there were gangs of gypsies going on the rampage in the city, breaking windows and looting, and destabilizing. The buses rolled into the city through the southern slums and got them all off at the end of the tramway line. The prison drivers said they didn't have the guts to go any farther than that. They told them the truth: Ceausescu had fled and demonstrators were flooding the city.

He left on foot. The trams were packed with people screaming their joy, waving flags with holes in the middle where the emblem used to be, singing "Olé, olé, olé!" He, too, burst into singing, "Wake up, Romanian," but all that came out was a groan that made the servants by the fire start. One of them came up and kicked him awake.

"Wake up, ye good-for-nothing stranger! How can you sleep and dream when death is watching you like a beast crouching in the bushes? Soon enough you'll go to sleep forever and there'll be plenty of sleep for you. Right now, you'd better stay awake and pray, for your end is near. Get ready for punishment! The master will soon be back down from the mountain."

He was all mixed up and took several minutes to realize where he was. The valley was bathed in shimmering moonlight. Perched on the cliffs, birds of the night shrieked piercingly and wild beasts sent in an indistinct murmur from afar. A gentle wind caressed his face.

Kneeling beside the camel to which he was tied, he took no further notice of the servants. He didn't care about their threats or the trial and punishment they said were going to follow. He knew that he should have no fear, only hope. He had been given a command and signs and in those signs he had to trust. He'd kept his spirit clean and hadn't craved for vanities. He'd had no lust for either the hot body of the woman or the glitter of gold and jewels of the goblet. He hadn't allowed his hand to become soiled by alien treasures or his spirit to be burdened with wanton love.

The servants' revelry was in full swing and their gleeful voices stirred up by wine echoed throughout the valley when a man all dressed in white holding a staff turned up near the fire emerging from the shadow of the rocks. The merrymakers froze and leaving food and drink aside bowed low and uttered with humility:

"Have mercy of your humble servant, master!"

The master touched them one by one with his ebony staff on their shoulders and they rose and surrounded him with lowered heads.

"We were not expecting you so early, wise Nabir," the head of servants ventured. "Do us the honor of joining our supper, for we are blessed with plenty of warm bread and fresh roast and celebrate this night the end of our journey which is now so close."

"Methinks I can already feel in the wind the fragrance of the spikenard with which the city courtesans bedaub their hair," one of the servants exclaimed making the others snicker.

The master chided the man for the coarse remark, while his eyes peered at the camels and donkeys resting by the fire.

"Where is the captive?" he asked.

"We tied him to a camel over there, so he should not escape," the guard said pointing at the place, wondering how come the master knew about the prisoner though none of them had said a word about him.

"Untie him presently and bring him to me," said the man called Nabir.

"Be careful, master. He is a robber and might be dangerous," a servant cautioned. "It must be he that robbed us back at the oasis. Look what we found on him." The man held out the bag and showed it to his master in the firelight so he might see it well and recognize it.

"Do not tarry! Untie him faster, foolish servants!" the master said in anger without casting a single glance at the bag, which they presented as evidence of the captive's guilt.

Presently, the servants removed the ropes and led him to the fire. No sooner had the master caught sight of him than he raised his hands above the flames and said in humble voice:

"Pray forgive my servants for any harm they may have done to you!" He added then, as an excuse: "I went up there in the mountains to examine the luminaries of the night, as I usually do whenever my caravan stops in an open place like this far from the din and lures of the city. These foolish men were I'm afraid incapable of giving you a decent reception."

"Bless you, wise man, and may the Lord my God forever bless your house and fortune!" he replied pressing his palms together before his chest and bowing humbly. "Here I am completely in your power and awaiting your right judgment."

"Why shall I judge you, righteous man?" the stargazer asked in surprise. "My foolish servants have wronged you all too much already, charging you with a crime that you had not committed. Earlier tonight, while I was gazing at the sky up there among the rocks, signs showed me you were coming to my camp and I returned as quickly as I could to greet you."

The servants listened gapingly to their master's speech, but seeing him kowtow and touch the dust before the man they had tied to a camel made them step back in fright. The stranger, too, was quite amazed and quickly put his hands on Nabir's shoulders and raised him saying:

"Please rise, wise man. I am not worthy of such honors. I'm nothing but a poor researcher, while you're a wealthy man. I travel across the wilderness on foot, while you have a rich caravan and servants and everything you want."

"You're right, righteous researcher, but I'd have nothing had I been fated otherwise. Besides, I'd gladly give up everything I have if this could help increase my knowledge and let my mind discover the great secrets of the world. Tonight, as I gazed at the stars above, I understood that Nineveh, my city, would be destroyed in retribution of our wickedness and pride. It grieved my heart, but at the same time I saw that there was hope. The luminaries of the night showed me the man that could redeem our city, as back in ancient times the prophet Yunus did, was lying tied up to a camel in my very camp."

"Oh, wise man, I dare not even think that what you say is true, although I must confess the purpose of my journey is to try and salvage the ancient writs, in which the science and wisdom of the world are shrined, from the disaster that will strike Nineveh. I have been given this order in the wilderness and I will have no rest until it is fulfilled."

Upon these words, the servants were filled with awe and fell down on their knees embracing his feet and begging him for forgiveness.

"Rise, brothers!" he said kindly. "Unless your bodies are still weary from the road, or the camels and donkeys cannot yet bear their burdens, let us lift this camp at once and hurry to Nineveh and warn the people there of the terrible danger looming on them."

"Indeed, let's move without delay," echoed the master of the caravan, but the servants were already packing and making ready for the journey and couldn't hear his words.

While they were still at it, the wise Nabir beckoned him to a nearby rock from the top of which the stars appeared so close as though they were about to climb down on the shoulders of the two men.

"Good researcher, it is important that you and I talk about something just the two of us. I know where it is what you are looking for. The tablets on which the ancient science and wisdom are inscribed are stored away in a safe place, but I'm afraid they too will perish if the city falls. They will be hard to hide so that our enemies can't trace them. Undoubtedly their warriors will leave no stone unturned and dig in every corner for the treasures they will assume were buried before their invasion. I therefore think you'd better help me save the entire city from disaster and so the tablets you have been charged to rescue will be saved as well.

"Wise man, I would be happy if the mighty Nineveh were spared the slightest harm. Indeed the writs themselves will thus be left unscathed. The voice that spoke to me in the wilderness, however, said Nineveh would be destroyed for the wickedness of the people that live within its walls and I believe the voice told me the truth. I fear we can't succeed no matter what we do."

"I think that there might be a way, my righteous friend. It is written that a mighty god turned from his fierce anger against the evil ways of Nineveh and spared the city in the ancient times. Yunus the prophet was sent to warn the Ninevites and urge them to repent and so they did. The king himself set the example, as he covered himself with sackcloth and sat down in the dust. The people of Nineveh believed that god's words and he, seeing their penitence, had mercy and did not bring upon them the destruction he had threatened."

"But I am not a prophet, wise Nabir. I am a poor researcher caught at a crossing of the ages and sent to wander in the wilderness. My words will never be so compelling as those of Yunus were. No kings will listen."

"I'll make them believe you are a prophet. I'll summon the rulers of the city to my court and tell them what the stars have showed me. I'll tell them you are the redeemer of Nineveh and they will believe me. I am one of the highest leaders of the city and I have never lied to them. Then you will strongly urge them to repent and they will do so and the city will once again be spared."

"Wise man, I'm sure you're all too well aware that our fragile human plans cannot prevent or sway what has been ordained and fated to occur. I fear it will all be useless; nonetheless I'll do what you want me to do, because I think it might be worth a try. But in return you'll have to take an oath that if the city, despite our efforts, is not saved, you'll take me to where the tablets are and help me rescue and preserve them for the centuries to come."

"I swear upon the luminaries of the night which help me glimpse into the future and in which I trust," the wise Nabir said unhesitatingly raising his right hand toward the starry sky.

They climbed down then and found the caravan ready to move. The servants gave him a camel free of any burden and they rode ahead of the convoy, Nabir and he, leading the way.

"To Nineveh! The city must be saved," the wise man cried out pressing his camel down the valley.

Some night birds darted from the rocks in fright. The moon was setting and the wind was blowing harder, sweeping away fine grains of sand.

4

THE INSTITUTE WAS GOING TO THE dogs. The pay was late and discontent was growing. The unions were staging protest actions and their leaders were up in arms. He did not have much confidence in union protests any longer. He'd had a taste of these tricks and wouldn't let himself be fooled again. He knew better than that.

Along with several other workmates he'd picketed the ministry for a few days. In his view, it was merely a scheme to put some people in the limelight. They'd been staying there with their placards under the scorching sun for hours on end. The ministry employees who passed by their small group would hardly cast a look on them like they were trash. Only some idle passers-by would stop and hang around once in a while. Some even cursed them loud because they occupied the sidewalk. Gypsy women with their usual knack for business walked round the group peddling roasted sunflower seeds. One of them, fumbling under her countless skirts, pulled out a bag of sun goggles and tried to make them buy some. They told her to get lost: they had no money. They hadn't got their paychecks for two months and that precisely was the reason why they were picketing the ministry. An old man with a ragged bag kept nosing around the group, trying to have a word with them.

"I've noticed you hanging out here for a few days. What's the matter? I reckon you are educated people, intellectuals. Why do you have to take to the streets like those bums at the University Square that messed up the whole city?"

"Listen, grandpa! How would you like they stopped sending your pension for a few months? Would it be all right with you?"

"Of course, not. Why should they cut off my pension? I've worked for it, didn't I?"

"So do we. We work for our pay, but they won't let us have it."

"This ain't right. Ain't right at all," the old man said shaking his head. This never happened in Ceausescu's day. Everyone got their wages. You see that we were better off back then?"

"Go fuck yourself, old fart!" one of the protesters burst out. "Get your Communist propaganda out of here!"

They'd come from the public television channel to film them. The cameramen found them torpid in the parching heat and said they couldn't put them on the air like that. They asked the protesters to shake their placards and yell for a few minutes, shot some pictures, then packed their stuff on their car and buzzed off.

The union demanded to see the minister, but he was nowhere to be found. The secretary said he was to the government. His deputy received them and listened to their plight, while he was checking his e-mail. Then he stood up and fed the fish in the aquarium but told them to go on all right, for he was listening. Finally, he apologized: he had to go. And anyway he had no way to help them. It wasn't he that carved the budget pie, he hinted, but said he'd talk it over with his boss and they would try to find some financing resources for the institute. It wouldn't be an easy job, though, because "the government, you know, has other priorities right now."

He considered writing an article and showing the quagmire in which Romanian research was caught, but who would care about it? People had other fish to fry. Food and fuel prices went up every week, while wages shrank and shrank. He thought he'd publish the article in some major foreign paper to make sure the ruling forces took it into account. He asked some colleagues for advice and soon enough the institute grapevine had it that he was going to send a memo to Strasbourg to rat on the authorities and censure their indifference. All sorts of people would drop by at the lab and encourage him to do so. Among them was a doubtful guy, a former local party boss turned union leader. One day, he showed up with a list. He was collecting signatures for yet another protest action of the union.

"I'm fed up with these protests. I'm not signing anything," he told the list man sternly.

"How come you of all people are not signing? You ought to be on our side. You are a noted personality. People know who you are. Why would you shy away right now?"

"I'm not shying away. I simply fail to see the point of protesting if no one gives a damn."

"This time we're doing something big, something that will catch the attention of the media, jolt the authorities out of their slumber. We're going to block the beltway right here, near the overpass."

"But that's against the law. The gendarmes might step in."

"Let them, we don't fear them," said the union man carried away by a revolutionary impulse he was apparently unable to restrain. "We will fight them, if we have to. Let the entire nation see how we researchers stand up for our rights. Look at the miners how they fought and won—"

"Look, man, I don't like this stuff. I'm a researcher not a punching bag for cops."

"Then you're a coward, sir, whatever people think about you at the institute. How can you stay away while your colleagues are fighting for our rights of us all that you yourself are going to enjoy?"

He let the big words suck him in and signed. The next morning he joined the other protesters at the gathering point outside Tower B. There was a big jumble out there, in which the organizers flurried handing out placards and instructions. Some of the protesters argued against the roadblocks. Others, by contrast, said they were necessary, or else the television crews were not going to come.

They walked the distance to the beltway in a quiet column like a dumb flock driven to pasture. It was already hot and it was going to be parching hot by noon. The protesters were lightly dressed; only some of the organizers wore some kind of topcoats—perhaps they'd been a little cool as they left home in the morning. The list man was heading the column. He appeared somewhat livelier than his troop, as he goaded them through a loudhailer and urged them to stick to their decision of blocking the road.

A group of sturdy guys that turned out to be protesters as well were already waiting under the overpass. The institute union leaders didn't know who they were. Only the list man seemed to know them and explained they were union members from the same trade 'branch' who'd joined the action out of solidarity.

He couldn't help glancing suspiciously at these 'branch' mates. A gray haired gentleman in a short-sleeved blue shirt appeared to be their leader. The action seemed well prepared indeed: a bunch of guys were unloading from a truck some metal fences that locked to one another through a sort of clicks. Two police cars came out of nowhere and blocked the traffic both ways. The 'branch' mates proved rather handy fellows. In no time at all, they put up the fences forming a corral that spanned the road. Meanwhile, the list man, a mighty skilful organizer, as he turned out to be, and the blue-shirted leader of the others climbed both of them on a heap of rubble from where they supervised the operations.

A Turkish truck driver kept bargaining with the organizers to let him pass. He had to arrive in Giurgiu as fast as he could, because his cargo he said was perishable and had already started to deteriorate during the long time they had spent in customs. But the organizers remained inflexible. The lines of cars waiting both sides of the roadblock were growing rapidly.

"Come on, please, come on everybody, get into the pen! Let's no one stay outside!" the loudhailer called.

The union members obediently complied entering one by one through the one narrow pass left open and heartened by the solidarity of their 'branch' mates, two or three voices started to shout, then they all chorused chanting, "Down-with-the-go-vernment! Down-with-the-go-vernment!" and "Thieves! Thieves!"

"Very well. Louder, louder!" the list man urged them on.

"All right! Start the pictures!" the blue-shirt man cried out. Several cameramen emerged from the car lines and started shooting.

"Now! Come on! Wave the placards! Chant!" the list man yelled into the loudhailer. "Down-with-the-go-vernment! Down-with-the-go-vernment!"

The cameramen were working. The din was at its highest pitch. Even the cars waiting along the road began to honk their horns. At that particular climax of labor struggle, he noticed that the guest demonstrators were one by one slipping beneath the fences and vanishing among the trucks that waited on the road. Also waiting under the overpass were two gendarmes vans that had gone unnoticed up to then. But now the riot troops fully equipped with shields and everything got down apace, lined up, and on command set off running toward the corral, which they swiftly surrounded on all sides. At this sight, the protesters' voices kind of broke; their slogans sounded lower and lower. Nothing exciting happened anymore. The heat had turned scorching.

"Stop the pictures! Pull out!" someone ordered. The cameramen obediently complied, packed their devices, and took off, while the demonstrators' fear was turning into sheer despair. The 'branch' buddies had made themselves scarce. They were alone in the pen and the gendarmes were tightening the noose, beating their shields with their rubber truncheons. No one was going to take pictures of what was to follow.

From where he stood close to a side of the corral he had a perfect view of the blue-shirted man on top of the rubble mound. That gentleman seemed to be the highest-ranking man around, since everyone obeyed his orders. Even the gendarme colonel, who sported a big mustache on his puffed up drunkard's face, had made him a salute and seemed to wait for the other's green light to start doing the job that he had come to do. He didn't realize who gave the signal: was it the man in blue shirt or the colonel? Turmoil broke out. The gendarmes charged, knocked down the fences, and fell on them from all sides, hitting them with their truncheons, while they pressed against one another, trapped and screaming. A few women had fallen down and the other protesters were trampling on them and the toppled fences, trying to get away.

A truncheon struck him heavily in the arm. He doubled up in pain and tried to lean on a fence but missed it and collapsed on the road. The nightmare went on above him: blows poured with muffled sounds; curses and screams jumbled into a roar. He didn't smart so much from the injury as from the humiliation of being hit again. He had seen the face of his assailer: this one was not a thug, much rather a backward kid, a country boy in gendarme uniform. He had struck with hate, gnashing his decayed teeth. Perhaps was he angry for being denied a furlough for a long time over these endless demonstrations. Or he was bugged that the daily ration of marmalade had spoiled his teeth and the girls wouldn't like him anymore.

He crawled among the gendarmes' legs trying to reach the border of the road. Rumpled old boots clattered around him. The gendarmes too were poor but had no way to protest. They followed their orders beating people around. A boot kicked him in the jaw. Perhaps he'd stared at it from too close and the boot didn't like it. Boots too can have their personality, their pride. The blow had made him reel. His jaw felt numb and he kept wondering whether the filthy, metal-tipped boot had not by chance peeled off his face and spread it on the road. He felt like he was tumbling in the dark, like in the old days when the Securitate beat him and it was as if time had stopped still and nothing had changed.

When he came to, he was lying on the grass by the ditch. An ambulance doctor was sticking a Band-Aid on his cheek packed with blood and road dust. He felt breathless and thirsty and asked for water, but it seemed there wasn't any. A Turkish driver, who took pity of him, fetched him a bottle with a stale yellow juice in it. Inside the broken pen, the pavement was littered with odd shoes, plastic bags, and purses. Rummaging through the remains, a stray dog had found something to chew—perhaps a sandwich or a croissant some protester had brought along in case he might get hungry demonstrating. They had no time to grow hungry. Shaking and bruised, they were shuffling up the road to Tower B, as to a benevolent giant, their protector.

The gentleman in the blue shirt was still there. He had climbed down the heap of rubble and was chatting with the chief of gendarmes. They were smoking and making fun of something. The 'branch' supporters were back, too, and were giving a hand to the gendarmes to clear the fences off the road. The colonel was patting his moustache with satisfaction as with a job well done. He shouted every now and then at his subordinates to make them scurry: they wouldn't keep him standing there all day, would they?

The two car lines were setting noisily, heavily into motion, past a traffic agent who was fussing around like a titmouse, flinging his arms in all directions. The doctor above him had packed his little bag and was waving at the ambulance driver to get ready.

"Leave him off, doc. He's fucking all right. Don't waste your time on him," said the blue shirt.

"Shame on you, murderers," he gasped through his teeth.

"Up yours, asshole! You'll learn not to block state roads anymore," the blue shirt blurted out, while he and the colonel, both of them grinning at him, got into a car and off they went. The doctor, too, rolled away in his ambulance and everyone got back to their businesses as if nothing had happened. He was alone, leaning on a fence in the shade, trying to pull himself together. The stray dog came sniffing around, hoping to get something to eat, but he had nothing, not even hope and felt more humiliated than he'd felt back when he crawled out of the thicket where the Securitate men had beat him on that same beltway. History was repeating itself, he thought, as he dragged himself away, stopping every few steps to rest. The villagers had come out to the gates and stared at him with curiosity. The rumor was out that the gendarmes had thrashed the institute trade union at the overpass.

At the bus stop outside the tower he ran into other protesters that had gotten away with only a few bruises. They were cursing furiously and said it had all been a setup, an excuse to have them beaten by the gendarmes and discouraged, but he didn't care. He felt like laughing and indeed burst out roaring with laughter as he passed by a pub and saw them: there they sat under a beach umbrella chatting over beers like old chums the mustached colonel of gendarmes, the man in blue shirt, and the list man. He laughed so loud that people began staring at him, and then suddenly he felt so sick that he had to cling to a tree and puke. When he could walk again, he returned to the lab.

*   *   *

He was through with union protests. It seemed to him everything was just a base scheme: the former union leaders who had goaded them to take to the streets and demonstrate, had become ministers and from the government looked down on them and jeered at the suckers they had used to climb up to the top. So many years after Ceausescu's overturn, things were still not improving. Actually, they were getting worse and worse and he kept wondering why until one night a dream gave him the answer he was looking for.

It was yet another stifling hot day. The institute was on vacation except for a few people, including him, that were still calling at the library in Tower B to look up books and articles they needed for their papers. He was keen on seeing a particular journal, which the library ladies said had been transferred to the basement rooms for storage. Moaning and groaning they had no time to look it up for him, they finally agreed to give him the key to go down there and find it by himself.

The man who they said was responsible for all the country's mess was right there in the storage room, a cubicle with a small barred window near the ceiling, very much like a prison cell. He was sitting on an iron-legged chair, gesticulating and grumbling restlessly, looking extremely upset. He had taken off his karakul cap and was banging it on the table at his side.

He had no idea who he was squabbling with, since there was no one else in the room. Judging by his embattled look and tousled hair, it seemed he'd just come out of a row. He couldn't figure out how the character had turned up in that storage room. He had died long ago—it had been in the papers and they'd even showed his execution on the tube. They'd shot him in Targoviste on Christmas many years back. People even said it was his Communist pals that did him in: anyone else would have had some respect and had recoiled from shedding blood the day the Lord was born.

He suspected it had been just another make-believe, some of their artfully stage-managed tricks. He wasn't dead since he was sitting there in the basement of Tower B where the Securitate once used to keep the listening devices through which they spied out what people were chatting in the labs. Or maybe he was just a ghost and found the place appealing. Maybe he'd sat there once and listened in the headphones the jokes that the researchers used to tell about him and liked them so much that he'd come back for more. Anyway, the character had hardly seen him walking through the door that he began to yell:

"What's going on here, comrade? Why is no one coming to work?"

"Well, it's vacation time— Myself— I'm only looking for a book I need," he said still stunned by that incredible encounter.

"What nonsense are you speaking, comrade? How can there be any vacations when the farming season is at its height? Where are your party leaders at the institute that they don't come to welcome me? Have they sent you in advance? What's your office in the local party bureau?"

"I don't hold any office. I've never held one. Actually, I was not even in the party," he said as though to justify himself.

"That's very bad! Very bad indeed, comrade. You should have got involved."

"You bet it was bad. That got me into all sort of troubles: I was denied any promotion, any traveling abroad. They even put me in the nuthouse when they didn't like what I was saying."

"You must have been a reactionary unworthy of the party's trust."

"Well, not exactly. I've always minded my own business, but it was they that wouldn't let me be."

Resting his karakul cap on the corner of the table, the character pulled up the sleeve of his overcoat, glanced at his watch, and then with the benevolent air of someone who is very busy, yet would spare a few minutes of his precious time to clarify a problem, he said:

"Look, I'm the secretary general and I believe we must sort this out. Let's take a look and see why you were not accepted in the party. What is your social origin? What were your parents: workers, peasants?

"Peasants. Quite simple folks they were, but they could notice I had some brains and they sent me to school."

"How many hectares did they own?"

"I don't know very well. Three or four acres I think."

"Did they join the collective farm of their own free will, or were they the kind that would run away from home and hide into the woods when our activists came over from the town to talk some sense into them?"

"They signed in right from the start, as far as I remember. They were scared they'd be run in, as one of our neighbors had been. No one has ever seen him since. Rumor had it that the Securitate shot him dead at the edge of some woods."

"There you are, comrade! This is the problem! They didn't do it out of conviction that a new life had to be built in the villages. They did it out of fear."

"That's true," he had to admit. "Hadn't they done so, they would have had no chance to see me or my brothers through high school. We would have been rejected."

"Now you see, comrade: the party has provided for your learning. The party has built schools. If it weren't for the party, there would have been no place to send you to. They would have kept you home to work in the fields and you had ended up to be exploited by the landowners and kulaks."

"Well, perhaps not for, you see, back in my village, it was he—the landowner, as you call him, sir—that would drop by the primary school every now and then, to inquire about the peasants' children and see that those who were more clever should be sent to school."

"Bullshit! You're lying," the secretary general all worked up cried out. "Landowners would never do such thing. They were exploiting people and even if they helped someone, they did so to the profit of their social class. You definitely have no proper political training, or else you wouldn't be talking such nonsense. Now, I see: This is the foremost reason why they didn't let you join the party."

"I grant you I don't take much interest in politics. That's why I've kept away from all political parties since the revolution."

"What revolution are you talking about? Revolution, my foot!" the character exclaimed and grabbing the karakul cap from the table furiously flung it against the floor. "This was no revolution, comrade: this was a coup. A coup plotted by traitors within the party in collusion with the spy agencies of foreign powers."

"I don't know very much about these things, but I think it was a revolution and a bloody one at that. Quite a lot of people were killed. I myself narrowly escaped getting a bullet through my head."

"You're mixing it all up," the secretary general cut in trying to calm down a bit. "The propagandists that were supposed to teach you apparently didn't do their duty. I'm going to explain it all to you myself. Now, look: The Marxist-Leninist doctrine and historical materialism have showed us that a revolution replaces an obsolete social system with a superior one. In Romania, back in 1989, it was the other way around. It was a counterrevolution, since Socialism, according to our Marxist theory, is a just and fair system, definitely superior to capitalism. Going back to capitalism with all that ensues is therefore nothing but an involution of society. Do you get it, comrade?"

He didn't answer. He'd climbed down to the storage room just to look up a journal, certainly not to listen to some hackneyed theories, but the secretary general was nowhere near to drop it. On the contrary, he'd set off on an impassioned revolutionary speech.

"Those who ousted me from power and had me executed were but traitors. They have betrayed and will continue to betray the interests of the people, as you can see out there. Do you think I don't know what's going on above? I've got my men all over the place, in every structure and they report it all to me. I used to organize the class struggle in the underground and I'm going to do it all over again. Although they had me shot and buried off by stealth, they are not rid of me. Actually, they did me a favor, as now I can much more easily creep into the people's minds and make them think what I want them to think and act accordingly. There will never again be any kind of market economy in Romania. I've seen to it that properties should stay forever, albeit in different ways, in the hands of the people's representatives. I have organized a widespread popular resistance. By night, I get into the workers' dreams and urge them to go on strike and sabotage, and kick out the capitalists who want to buy the factories our people built by the sweat of their brows."

"You shouldn't do such things, sir," he tried to make him understand. "There will be no future for this country. It will become a hopeless case."

"Please stop calling me 'sir'. This is a retrograde way of addressing people that we have long banned from our language. You shall call me 'comrade', the same as I am calling you." Then he relented a little bit and asked: "What's your profession, comrade?"

"I'm a researcher, sir, or rather I used to be a researcher at this institute. Now I'm as good as jobless, since the ministry has no money for us and we come to work for nothing. I mean we don't get paid. The state can no longer afford—"

The secretary general saw red again:

"They have wrecked everything, these traitors. I had created a real small town of physics here, in which scientists and workers were supposed to work and learn and live together. It was a prototype of how we were going to connect education and research and production into one. In terms of living standards, it was a model of how the multilaterally developed Socialist society and Communist society later on were going to look like. It was Communism in the bud in fact. What has become of this place? Where are the small-lot production units? Where are the top-notch nuclear devices the factory was turning out? Do you think I don't know? The factory was sold for peanuts. The foreign made lathes, for which our people toiled and saved foreign exchange, were cut to pieces and melt down, and the workers—laid off, all of them. What view do the researchers take of this?"

"There are not many researchers left, sir. The older ones have retired and the younger have moved or hope to move abroad."

The secretary general angrily smashed his fist down on the table:

"What about the comrade activists? They were supposed to guide research activity. Where are they?"

"They— how shall I put it?— they, as expected, were the first to go into business: one opened up a store, another a garage or a small factory, you know—"

"Traitors!" the secretary general burst out. "I have invested politically and financially in them and now they turn into promoters of counterrevolutionary capitalism. They're a discredit to the party."

"Truly, sir, they are a bunch of opportunists. How convincingly they spoke about the party manifesto! What solemn commitments they were making and such high political training they used to have!"

"Traitors, renegades," he murmured and dropped his hand in disappointment. "But at least our education system that trains our future cadres must be working fine, since I provided everything they needed on this campus. Now, tell me, how is education here these days?"

"Bad! They closed down the physics high school and the faculty itself is going to the dogs. If it goes on like this, shortly enough we'll have no specialists at all and research will be out for good."

"I see. It's worth than I imagined," he said shaking his head with bitterness. "I'll have to struggle a lot to put it right, but I am not afraid. I've faced the prisons of the landowners and bourgeoisie and the bullets of traitors within my own party. What about you? You seem to be a frank and honest comrade. Why are you sitting on your hands? Come on! Join our struggle for the just cause for which I'll fight relentlessly. I will enroll you in the party right away if you like. I can do that, for I'm the secretary general."

"No, thanks. I'm not interested. Actually, I'm not interested in the restoration of Socialism either," he replied and started looking for his journal. "Clearly, this country will never ever go back to what it used to be."

The secretary general hushed him up with an expert smile:

"You're dead wrong, comrade. I advise you, as I advised every one of my collaborators, to have patience until the historical conditions are ripe for the return of Socialism in Romania and all over the world. I don't mind saying it all over again to make myself clear. Marxist theory, historical and dialectical materialism have shown that quantitative accumulation leads to qualitative leaps. People want Socialism back again—I'm positive about that. They talk about me every day. Do you have any idea what our Maramures peasants say in their folk songs these days? Listen to this: 'Communism ain't gone for good; / It's still in the neighborhood. / Ceausescu he ain't dead: / He just went to take a nap.' You see? It's a wonderful sample of the creative spirit of our people who in their folk songs voice their aspirations toward freedom and justice. It is an unambiguous proof they want me back and that's why I'm haunting all over the country and you can see my shadow everywhere. You can see how the workers listen to me and refuse to work for the owners. The miners stage strikes and uprisings when I tell them to. And the peasants have chased the landowners that claimed back their estates."

"Frankly, I hope with all my heart you'll fail and we'll never have to return to the darkness from which we have emerged. Although I'm now in a tight spot because my pay is two months late, I think this country will be all right in the end. In my view, the Romanians live in poverty because Communist rule for decades smashed up everything, including their capacity for normal thinking."

"How can you talk this way, comrade?" the secretary general said in a slighted tone of voice. "We wanted to create a new man with a high degree of conscience, free from the selfishness that private property engenders. That's why production means belonged to the entire people. We put up apartment buildings, hospitals, schools, and kindergartens. We wanted to wipe off the difference between villages and cities."

"Yeah, I could see that. You wanted to turn the cities into dark villages, and the villages into desert fields covered with heaps of rubble and haunted by howling hungry dogs abandoned by their masters."

"Not at all, comrade. You are wrong again. We wanted to build modern residences for the peasants and restore to agriculture the lands uselessly occupied by their ineffective households. We can't make the territory of the country larger than it is, can we? We therefore need to make the best of it. You're a researcher, you can calculate: In a ten-story block standing on two-three hundred square meters, we were able to house 30 to 40 families of peasants whose households would otherwise have sprawled across nearly five hectares. The crop from these cleared lands, if sold abroad, would have fetched substantial revenues. Besides, the peasants would not have stolen any longer. Living in blocks of flats they would have needed no more grain or corn. In the morning, the heads of stairways would have read the roll call, ordered them into columns, and led them to work. Everything down to the finest detail was well planned. For good results incentives would have been provided. The most effective workers would have received food stamps of a certain color entitling them to higher caloric meals at the district canteen. On their free days they would have even got permits to visit neighboring colonies and share their work experience. They would have been provided both overalls and Sunday clothes to wear at cultural and educational events. The children would have been raised and educated all together in nurseries and kindergartens where parents and relatives would have been allowed to visit them according to a schedule without having to waste on them any of their working time which in agriculture, as you must know, since you're a peasant's son, extends from dawn to dusk."

"But this is a sort of slavery," he burst out in outrage.

"Wrong, wrong, comrade," the secretary general countered. "You obviously have no idea about historical materialism. What I was planning to achieve was the very highest form of social organization. I was laying the groundwork for a new society in which the common good would have triumphed over mean egotistic interests once and for all. It is within this frame alone that man can freely work and create for society, which in turn distributes to everyone according to his needs and asks from everyone according to his abilities. This was my ideal and I would have led Romania to a new acme of civilization if the traitors hadn't mounted a coup and shot me."

"There is something I fail to grasp. You say they shot you. I know they shot you, so how come I can still be talking with you?"

"It's easy: I've been dead for quite a while, but I still live in every Romanian's mind, particularly when someone is disgruntled. No one can see me unless they want to. You can see me yourself because I am still there inside your mind and you desire to see me."

"You must be right to some extent I reckon."

"I'm telling you as I've been telling the current leaders of the country: Keep the spirit alive until the conditions for the return of Communism are ripe. Pay but lip service to this market economy rubbish, which is entirely wrong. I see they're wise and take heed of my words."

He was astonished: "You mean to say you're still talking to them after they shot you, slandered you, and siphoned away the money from your bank accounts?"

"They did want to hurt me all right, but I bear no grudges against anyone; not when the future of Socialism and Communism is at stake. I keep visiting them while they are sleeping. I talk to them, give them advice, and they listen to me, particularly the one who's in command right now. He's got solid political training, knows his Marxism to the dot. That's why I bear with him. I could put him into big trouble right away if I liked. I could sneak into the engine of his plane and blow it up, or put a spell on one of his security guards. They're all my children and my pupils and none of them would disobey. But I don't want to hurt him. It doesn't suit my purposes. What if his successor doesn't listen to me? My whole work of steering people back to Communism would go down the drain. It nearly happened when that bearded professor was allowed to lead the country. Although he'd been a party secretary in my day, his Marxism and dialectical materialism were shallow. He'd hardly seen himself at the top that he imagined he was on his own, paid no attention to me, and came close to ruining my plans. He wanted to give up the country to capitalists for real. Fortunately, I was there and talked to those concerned and showed them how to smear and unsaddle him. He had already started to spoil the people's minds, teaching them his phony capitalist democracy. With those who are in power today, it's different: I get along with them."

"So much the worse for you. I thought you were on the people's side but I was wrong. How can you be satisfied with today's rulers? I think they're greedier than vultures. They go on slapping taxes on the people and alienate those who have swept them into power."

"It's true; they're only after money and have forgotten all about the code of Socialist fairness and ethics they used to learn by rote back when they were applying for party membership. But you must know that I encourage them along this road. Let them be greedier and greedier and make nothing but blunders. That suits me perfectly and benefits the people.

"What do you mean?"

The secretary general looked disappointed: "You're no good when it comes to politics. It's very easy, comrade. The rulers by their conduct must make the people loathe market economy and capitalism and wish for the return of Communism. This is our deal: that they should compromise the sham democracy of capitalism and in exchange I'll see that they still be in power when the comeback happens. When fortune turns, they know better than anyone how to land on their feet. They've given abundant proof of it. I know I can depend on them."

Two creatures with covered faces suddenly came into the room.

"Hey, you! Break's over! Back to task!" Upon these words, they lifted the secretary general by the armpits and vanished through the wall towards the sewers.

"Remember, comrade," he could still yell as the wall swallowed him. "As long as my ghost still lurks in the Romanians' minds, nothing good will happen to this country. And you won't shake me off so easily."

"Enough! Get lost! Leave us alone!" he shouted back in anger and flung behind the fading ghost the ring of keys that he was holding.

"Whom are you arguing with, sir?" asked the librarian reprovingly. Her eyes were searching the small room for some hidden intruder while he was still furiously staring at the wall before him. "I've told you that you were not to bring anyone along. We let you come down here unaccompanied only because we've known you for all these years and trust you, but we have our responsibilities. Should any books be missing, we must pay—"

He was quite straightforward about it and tried to tell her the whole story, but she had hardly heard a few words that she dashed up the stairs and returned with the chief librarian who soothingly, but more or less directly urged him to go and see a shrink again. Such things happen with this summer heat and all, she said.

*   *   *

He had been dreaming of the secretary general almost every night since then. He was very displeased with what was going on at the institute and took it out on him as though he was responsible for it.

"I wanted to make a unique experiment, build a strong center that would intermingle education, research, and production. And what's it coming to? You've made a mockery of it. I will dismiss you all and send you work on farms and building sites."

"There's no one left for you to fire," he kept telling his visitor. The older researchers have gone into retirement. The younger ones are moving abroad wherever they can find a place."

"This is intolerable, comrade!" the secretary general cried out. "We must not let them buy our people's brains away. I'll order that everyone that works in research be stopped at the border and turned back to their jobs."

"You can do no such thing. We're free now. Everyone can go anywhere he likes. Provided he's got the money. It's no longer like it used to be. You forget there's been a revolution."

"I've told you a thousand times: This was no revolution. This was a coup plotted by traitors!" yelled the other.

Every now and then, he remembered to ask about the energy issue:

"What about that new method for generating energy without consuming any fuel? Where are the comrade researchers that have pledged to develop it by the next congress of the party? I have invested money and more in them and they deceived me. I'll teach them a lesson. Just wait and see what's gonna happen to you all. Researchers, are you not? I'm gonna cut you off without a penny!"

He would wake up in fright and light the lamp on the nightstand and every time from somewhere very close, such as the wardrobe, the secretary general shouted like mad:

"Turn off the light, comrade! We can talk in the dark as well. With what you're burning a loom can operate and produce extra goods for export."

One night the visitor came up with a proposal. He was speaking softly for a change, trying to coax him into going away, since anyway there was nothing left for him at the institute. They could be partners, he said, prowling around, creeping into the people's minds, and prompting them to bring back Communism. All he had to do was turn into a ghost like he was, wheedled the secretary general offering him a glass in which he said was poison.

Fortunately, a hoary-bearded man, wearing a priestly-like black tunic, suddenly turned up and scolded the secretary general. The apparition grabbed the glass from his hand, flung it against some rock, and calling him an evil ghost drove the obnoxious visitor away.

The priest or whatever he was then turned to him and said:

"Don't waste your time talking to fools, nor sell your soul to the evil one. Walk on the road of the righteous and seek the peace of your heart."

"How shall I do that?" he asked.

The black-clad man opened a leather bag with various papers, selected one that was rolled like a parchment, and said:

"These numbers will open up the road for you and show you how far you are from the place of truth. He who has eyes, let him see; he who has ears, let him hear; he who is wise, let him understand."

The man handed him the scroll on which he could see a sequence of numbers. He read them in his dream and apparently memorized them, for when he woke up later on he was able to write them down in his notebook in the same order as they were written on the scroll. He first thought they could be his lucky numbers, those that would change his life: he could bet on them in the lottery and win, become financially independent. Taking a closer look, he realized they were geographical coordinates and very precise ones, such as a satellite-corrected system would provide them. He searched his atlases and maps and found they pointed to an area around a remote cloister located by a river in the woods.

He had no time to waste. At dawn, he packed a knapsack with his maps and compass and a few other things and off he went.

He took a train up to the station that he found was nearest to his destination, then he pursued his trip by bus, a nearly empty, battered vehicle. The driver noticed the way he fumbled through his maps and asked:

"Whereto, boss?"

"I'm going to a cloister down the road," he replied pointing to a place he had highlighted on the map. The driver needed no map to know what he was talking about.

"You mean you're looking for the Father Researcher, aren't you? Come sit by me. I'll tell where you must get off."

He moved into the seat next to the driver, while the bus turned slowly onto a potholed road. He kept thinking about the driver's words. A 'father researcher' sure sounded like someone special, someone he would like to meet. Since the driver looked like a talkative guy, he seized the opportunity to pry a little further:

"Do you know the Father Researcher?"

"Know him? Of course I know him, sir. We're even friends, I'd say. He's got lots of gizmos, knows awfully many things. He does his research out there in the woods. Myself, you know, I was not up to much in school, but when the Father told me about antimatter and the plasmoids, I got his point. Particularly as I had serious trouble with the plasmoids myself."

He was quite amazed: "What trouble could you have with a plasmoid. It is a rare phenomenon that never appears except in very special conditions."

Puffing at a cigarette stuck at the corner of his mouth, the driver focused on averting the potholes, but this didn't keep him from spinning out the story.

"The plasmoids truly exist, sir. They gave me a lot of trouble and I've been telling this story ever since to anyone who'd listen, so that they know about them and be on their guards. I was going to the cemetery to weed out some apricot shoots, you know, that crowded out old grandpa's tomb and fix the cross. T'was a shame to let it go to seed like this. People were talking. They said we didn't care 'bout him and never went uphill no longer to light a candle or anything and trees were growing over him, poor soul. Lice nearly ate him alive in the war. And what for, can you tell me? A few acres, that's what he'd struggled for. No sooner had he got his land after the war than they took it away from him during the collectivization. Now, with this democracy and all, they've given it back to me, as his only grandson, you know, though it ain't the same land: it's a different plot elsewhere, 'cause they said it's the law: acres is acres everywhere. But never mind that. So I took a hatchet and a hoe and a pail of cement, put them in the wheelbarrow, and here I go honkle-bonkle to the cemetery. I did what I had to do, wrapped it all up by sunset, packed my things back in the wheelbarrow, and headed home whistling like a robin. Once I got there, I started putting everything away in the shed and then guess what? The hatchet was missing. I'd left it back at grandpa's. So I said to my woman, 'Woman, I've left the hatchet at the cemetery. I think I'd better go after it.' 'You bet you do, or else it'll be gone just like the other one the gypsies pinched as they came tin the soap pail, may they cut off their fingers with it!' T'was night already, but with a big full moon up there, the road was shining almost like in broad daylight. I had taken my searchlight anyway, just in case I had to look for the damn hatchet among those graves, since I didn't remember where exactly I had left it. As I was walking into the cemetery, I ran smack into the little Father. 'Good even, Father,' said I. 'Bless you, my son,' said he and went on, such as how I was lately and what I was doing there at night. 'Coming to collect my hatchet—I left it somewhere around here.' 'Take care, son! There are plasmoids all over the place. God forbid, you may pick one up and take it home with you.' 'What do you mean 'plasmoids'?' I asked as I remembered the village folks were talking about ghosts. You see, we had another priest here before the Father Researcher: he didn't care 'bout anything except banging the people's women until they caught him and beat him stiff and chased him from the village. But then, you know, after a while, people started to talk the dead he'd buried didn't get proper service and were not at peace. Folks said they were lurking among the graves especially on full moon nights like that one. So I asked the Father whether he meant zombies or such stuff, but he said no, t'was something else. Charged with negative energy he said it was and having mechanical effects. I'm a bit of a mechanic myself, so I kind of saw what he meant. They called it a plasmoid, he said. Scientists did."

The driver cut off his story at that point. He'd caught up with a file of rickety, patchily covered wagons riding right in the middle of the road. He honked a few times, but the gypsies had no intention to make room, which set him swearing. It was a graphic, unusually prolix curse involving the gypsies' mothers, grandmothers, and so on, for generations. He calmed down slowly once he had overtaken the wagon file. It showed on his face he was sorry having to interrupt his story, because some louts just didn't care that there were other people besides them in the world and had taken possession of the road ahead of time.

"Same as a car battery, the Father said they were," he suddenly resumed after a silence, "the plasmoids, all charged with negative energy and once they bumped into some other thing full with positive charge, pop, they got discharged and some mechanical effect happened. I thought to myself he was reading too much, so I went to the tomb and there stood my hatchet waiting for me, and by then I'd forgotten everything he said, but he was right: some of those bugs must have clung to me. I got home with my hatchet all right and felt I could do with a beer so I hopped into my Dacia to go fetch some from the village, but it wouldn't start. I got off take a look at it. I've told you: I'm good at cars. My Dacia, I can dismount it down to the smallest parts and mount it back blindfolded. I checked the fuel, looked at the ignition—everything was okay, only the damn thing wouldn't move. I gave up. The next day was a Sunday and the bus had no rides, so I took the car apart and guess what? The camshaft was broken as if it were a leek stalk, not a piece of iron. I got another one from a cousin of mine and while I was replacing it, still pissed and puzzled, the little Father came down the road from mass. 'What are you doing, son?' he said chidingly. 'Fixing the car on a Sunday instead of coming to church?' 'Sorry, Father, but what was I to do? Can you believe this? It conked out last night all of a sudden.' 'What's wrong with it?' 'The damn camshaft broke like a twig.' 'Don't swear, son, for the Old Nick has nothing to do with it. It's the plasmoid. You should have listened to me last night. You picked up the plasmoid at the cemetery and it wrecked your car.'"

He couldn't help smiling at the scientific conclusion of the driver's mishap. He wondered whether the Dacia carmakers were not more likely responsible for that broken shaft than the plasmoid the Father Researcher had chalked it down to. He had no time to utter his doubts aloud as the bus drew up suddenly in the middle of nowhere.

"There you are, boss. This is where you get off. 'Three Cobs'—that's the name of the stop, so you know where you want to get off next time you come here. You find the cloister by the brook, beyond that wood."

He took a dusty road by a parched pasture where a small herd of skinny cows were grazing. Across the pasture was a canal filled with clear water and lined with artesian wells the jets of which glittered brightly in the midday sun. There were seven fountains—he counted, as he went to quench his thirst to the nearest and tallest of them all, which was surrounded by a sunbow. He found the herdsmen—two sunburnt frail boys—sitting beneath the shrubs at the edge of the woods. They had untied the strings of their bags and were taking lunch, both biting heartily from lumps of cold polenta and wilted cucumbers they dunked into gross salt.

"Hi lads. Have a good meal!"

"Thank you, sir. You're very kind," they mumbled through their gulps.

"Are those cows yours?"

"Ours, sir. That is, the village folks'. We're only looking after them 'cause it's our turn."

"Do they still give any milk with this drought?"

"Oh no, sir! How could they?" one of the boys said shaking his head in sadness. "It's just too scorching hot. The pasture's all worn-out. There's nothing left for them to chew out there, poor things."

"Besides," the other one cut in, "folks torment them still worse, making them pull the plough, 'cause they have no oxen and hiring tractors, they say, is too expensive."

He took out a chocolate bar from the knapsack and offered it to the boys. Mighty pleased they were. They broke it into halves, shared it, and started munching happily right away.

"Thank you, sir. That's real charity you did. We needed something to sweeten our mouths after those bitter cucumbers. I haven't eaten chocolate in a long time. How about you?" he asked the other one, who shook his head and went on munching. "They do sell chocolate in the village at the private shop, but it's expensive and we've got no money." Plunging his hand down to the bottom of his bag, the boy took out a fistful of sunflower seeds. "Please have some of our polly seeds. They're good to crunch and if you drink some water after them, they make your tummy swell like you ate seven meals and keep hunger at bay. We do so when we're hungry, don't we?" the boy asked his companion who nodded in agreement.

He accepted the gift, put the seeds into his pocket, and asked the boys to show him the way to the cloister. One of them accompanied him up to a path in the woods.

"You follow this path to the brook, sir, cross the log bridge, and you'll see the cloister. You'll find the Father there. He never comes to the village except in the evening. He spends the whole day there doing experiments."

"What kind of experiments?" he inquired.

"I don't know, sir. I'm too young to know these things, but he's got something looking like a big dish on a pole, which folks say is an antenna to watch American TV."

Leaving the boys to their troubles, he followed the path through the wood. The air was cooler there and birds were twittering. When he arrived at the river, he skipped the bridge and, taking off his shoes, crossed dabbling through the water, as he had not done for a long, long time. The cloister, as the boys had told him, was quite close: its spire could be seen through the acacias that had overgrown the place. The Father Researcher was sitting on the porch of his cell working on a laptop that was supplied by a solar panel on the roof. The dish antenna was fastened on a mast next to a shed beneath which stood a ready-saddled horse nibbling some grain.

"Welcome, my friend," the Father greeted him and rose from the oaken bench on which he sat to meet him. With his short-trimmed hoary beard and his black tunic all buttoned up, the man resembled strikingly the vision that had driven the secretary general out of his nightmare.

"Father, I had a dream, you know," he stammered at a loss for words, as he had no idea what he was supposed to say.

"You don't need to explain anything," the other cut him in, as though he knew everything already, then silently examined the piece of paper the visitor was offering him instead of further introduction. On it were the few numbers he had jotted down after his dream.

"My friend, you have a problem," the Father said pensively after a while. "Like me, you are in search of the truth, but you have taken a different, more tortuous path. You're still at the same stage as most common researchers are."

"I don't think I know what you mean," he said.

"You'll know when the time comes and you'll join the researchers of the new century provided that you find the right path."

"I'm an experienced researcher, Father, and have obtained every degree that scientists my age may be expected to attain."

"I know you did, but those degrees are not much help to you right now. You are a good professional—I know that, too. You seem surprised, but the fact is I've known you for many years, actually since the time you were a physics student and came to do practical work in my laboratory. Back then, I was a young physicist myself."

"So you're a physicist yourself," he said even more astonished.

"I am. I've studied physics among other things and was a researcher for a good many years myself."

"Then how come you've turned into a priest? I hardly see how these professions can be reconciled with one another. Religious faith has always clashed with science and there have even been major disputes between the two of them."

The Father bade him to sit on the bench on the vine-shaded porch and said:

"Knowledge and faith, my friend, can't go without each other, for you can't know anything unless you believe. The human mind has temporarily separated them and it is also our mind that must bring them together back again, because the time has come to do so. We know nothing except what we are meant to know and would discover nothing unless the One who has created everything allowed us to do so. We pride ourselves on bringing forth new things, but they have always been there ever since the beginning. We simply haven't seen them, as we were not permitted to do so. The laws that physics, chemistry, biology, and all the other sciences have discovered have always existed, but the human mind only found them with great difficulty after much groping in the dark. I am appalled at the enormous ignorance in which mankind is trapped. What reason has discovered up to now is just a spark from the huge blaze surrounding us. It was this blaze of light and wisdom that prompted me to give up my research position, study theology, and move to this cloister in order to press on with my research but in a different way and on a higher level of knowledge. The exact sciences now seem to me impotent because they've shed their sacral nature. It will be up to the new century researchers to restore holiness to science, or else mankind will forever stumble on a sort of barrier that blocks the road to real knowledge. We will continue to take pride on moving the barrier a further step away on this great road the end of which we'll never reach."

"I must confess that I myself have felt for some time that research has reached an impasse. I recognize my limits and have got used to the idea, thinking that those who will be coming after us will obtain better results and find out more than we know."

"They'll find out more and grow increasingly frightened grasping that they're in fact bogged down in the complete unknown. Unless they find a new approach to research, they'll only deepen the chasm of unknown that surrounds them and end up in an existential crisis. It is imperative a new approach be found. As I was telling you, my friend, science has been desacralized and will have to be sacralized again. New century researchers will have to put faith before reason and theological virtue before the inquisitive mind. The true road will not become unveiled or open before their eyes until they do so."

"Specifically what are they supposed to do?" he asked feeling a real, growing interest in the subject.

"I guess you are, as any scientist of our times, a computer user and know, as we all do, that computer software cannot be used unless you secure the agreement of its creator. And aren't there tough laws to punish software piracy?"

"Of course, there are. One may even go to jail over it."

"In these conditions, I wonder what punishment we, scientists, deserve for neglecting or refusing to seek the Maker's permission for using the entire infrastructure of laws we, knowledge-thirsty men, commonly use in our studies. Any researcher planning to use a physical law to make a new discovery should say a prayer and request the Creator's permission beforehand."

He liked what he heard and felt everything around him was starting to make sense. He realized it was high time he made some changes in his life as a researcher, so he told his host:

"Look, Father. I'm a researcher crushed between two centuries. In the past century, I was oppressed and fettered. In the new one, I can't help feeling scorned and humiliated. No one needs us, researchers, unless we discover things that will fetch lots of money to those that are in control of our lives. I feel what you've just said is starting to enlighten me. If possible, I would like to become a researcher of the new century, guided by the truth."

The Father stood up and said:

"Welcome aboard, my son! Follow me!"

He followed the Father who stopped before the church porch, raised his arms and said in a thundering voice:

"This is the House of the Lord! The voice of our prayer is heard all across the Universe and faith can lift us to the skies. There is no man-made sophisticated system or equipment that can help us achieve this and any researcher must therefore enter the House of the Lord with humility, aware that human thinking power is limited, and leave behind him the delusive pride that makes us believe we are omniscient."

They walked into the church together. It was cool inside and their steps resounded on the flagstones. A pure wax candle was burning in a candlestick. As the daylight trickling in through the small windows was growing dimmer, the Father took the candle from the holder and kept it close to the pulpit walls on which gaunt-faced saints were painted.

"Look at these Holy Fathers!" he said. "They were all scholars who possessed the scientific knowledge of their day. They were researchers of their centuries who reached the utmost level of perfection through their faith. Today's science cannot account for, nor can we equal, a knowledge as advanced as theirs. They went through fire and were not burnt, trod on venomous snakes unharmed, walked on the water as we walk on solid ground and were not drowned, floated on air, and passed through walls and rocks. We are of course inclined to look for scientific reasons for their exploits, which nonetheless defy rational understanding. It took faith, fast, and prayer, and struggle against sin to do their deeds, but when their spirit doubted and their faith wavered, their powers were weakened, and this is something we must bear in mind."

He listened intently. He'd never heard anyone speak like that before and he felt sorry for having squandered so much time before he'd learned all this. He definitely felt he'd spent a lot of time to no avail. He used to think research couldn't be conducted except in institutes devoted to this purpose, in labs provided with top-notch equipment, but he now realized he had been wrong.

"Father," he said, "I am a self-taught man in many respects and I have always learned quite rapidly what I desired to learn. I guess I'll have to read a lot of books. Please tell me which books I need. Where can I find them?"

"Many things that you need to learn and know can be found in a book concerning the lives of the Holy Fathers I've been telling you about. Examine it as closely as you can. It's only in this way that your spirit will become enlightened and you'll make your first steps towards true knowledge." While he was saying so, he went up to a shelf and picked one of several large leather-bound tomes and handed it to him.

"This is the fundamental book of every knowledge seeker," the Father said so loud that the church walls echoed. "Endeavor to become a new century researcher rather than stay forever at the turn of the century!"

He took the book demurely and felt as though a thunderbolt was ripping through his being. The Father Researcher told him as he took his leave:

"When you feel like talking to me, whether to seek some advice or request an explanation, you'll find me here at the cloister. In fact, we will be able to keep in touch by e-mail. My PC is connected via satellite. From my place in the middle of this woods I'm striving to learn as many things as I can of those the human mind has been allowed to know."

He went straight home and, as he studied the book he had received, his life was switching to a different course. He understood that all human concerns were vain except the quest for truth, as had been proved in ancient times by those holy men, researchers of their centuries, whose lives were described in the book. But he lived in the world and had to struggle most of the time with its turmoil and human weaknesses.

5

HE'D SEEN A YOUNG QUINCE TREE in the fields almost collapsing with the weight of heavy fruit. Popular wisdom held this meant a long hard winter was about to follow. He'd warned them Tower B shouldn't be left without heating supply, but the managers were rather haughty people who didn't set much store on common wisdom.

"Come on, you're a researcher, sir, stop fooling around with such nonsense. Now that we have weather forecasts based on satellite data, believe me, it's a shame."

"No, listen to me, it will be colder than you can imagine. It's gonna be the hardest of all winters. The last winter perhaps—"

"Would you be serious, sir! Now, leave us if you please: we've got a meeting of the scientific council to attend."

It was stifling hot and, as he went around warning about the frost to come, some listened patiently, knowing the "institution" he had been to for a while. Others mocked his forebodings and suggested he should start canning the summer heat and store it for the winter. No one had ever done such thing: he'll surely win the Nobel Prize, they said.

The ministry officials were for some reason pissed with the institute and kept trimming down their budget allocations. To cap it all, their chief accountant had quit and their bill arrears had piled up so high that the gas people came over and cut off supply to their heating station. He was growing increasingly concerned and went on pestering the managers about, it but they didn't seem to care.

"Mister manager, sir, this is no kind of joke. The tower will have no heating. You need to take some steps."

"It's no business of mine. It ain't my tower. We're tenants here. Go tell the institute that owns the building."

The institute that owned the tower was headquartered on the next floor. Their general manager was hard to find because he was the one in charge of awarding research projects to everybody else. He talked with the secretary and registered for an audience. When he finally got it, he didn't cut much ice.

"The tower belongs to us indeed. We did agree on that when assets were divided, but every tenant institute has to take care of its utilities."

"It will be a disaster, sir. Water is dripping in the elevator: a short circuit may happen anytime. The library is dank like a cave. The journals have started to mold. God forbid that a flood occurs!"

"It's not my business to mend the tenants' broken pipes. I've got a record of how the space was when they rented it, so I don't care."

"What about the heating problem? How will the place be heated in the winter?"

"We'll figure out something. Don't you bother! Anyway there's still plenty of time until next winter."

When the winter did come, employees filled the chilling tower with the crankiest heating contraptions one would ever dream of, blowing the fuses every other minute, so that Mr. Tomescu, the chief electrician, and his team could hardly keep the pace, fixing broken connections and replacing the wires that were melting in the walls.

A cutting wind, presage of a nasty blizzard, had started to blow. He was on his way to see the manager and warn him once again that worse was still to follow, but he was out of luck: the elevator broke down and he was trapped inside more than an hour. After some guys with iron bars had pulled him out and he arrived all rumpled and disheveled at the manager's office, the manager himself was out as usual: he had grown wary of these visits and would rather avoid them as often as he had a chance.

On Christmas Eve, as the institute was closing for the holidays, he tried to see the manager again. He'd done some calculations on what would happen to the tower if it stayed unheated and had come to some grim conclusions. Inside, they were all partying over hard drinks and sausages.

"Bug off, man! Give us a break with your temperature gradients and stuff. Tower B is all right. What do you think will happen to it?" a management official exclaimed, then invited him to have a snack with them. "Come on, have a bite, there's enough for everyone."

He would not share their lavish lunch, for it was Christmas Eve, he said, and he was fasting. Some laughed and teased him on his penitence, so he just went away and left them alone.

Unfortunately, he was right. By the Epiphany when they returned to work, the tower was a dreadful wreck. The water pipes had burst up flooding several stories then the freeze came, so it now looked like a new glacial period had begun there, particularly in the library. Marvelous icicles—he hadn't seen such beauties since childhood when they amazed him on the eaves of his parents' house—hanged from the shelves girding with ice belts the books that now seemed fragile and powerless for all the valuable science they contained. The nuclear particles themselves lay stiff between their frozen pages; the electrons were finally at rest, unable to wander on their orbits any longer. Every single object was caught in ice—an eerie view it was and yet more beautiful than anything he had ever seen or imagined.

He had come for a book, but couldn't take it from the shelf at present for it was trapped within a block of ice. All he could see was the title on its cover enlarged as through a magnifying glass.

"I'm sorry to disturb you, madam, but I would like to have that book."

"Leave me alone, sir. Can't you see what's happened here?" the chief librarian snapped at him.

"It seems to me that you don't understand. I'm a researcher and I need the information provided in that book. Mine is a key profession and I insist that I be given appropriate priority, no matter what the circumstances."

"And I am a librarian, sir, and my profession is certainly older and perhaps not less important than yours," she retorted. "Ever since ancient times there have been great libraries in different areas of the world, in which librarians like us were doing their jobs. Physical research as a trade appeared I believe considerably later. I do not wish to argue with you. You know we've always gladly met any request of yours and will continue to do so, but not right now. I can't give you any book right now."

"Shall I come back tomorrow? Will you give it to me tomorrow?"

"I can't promise you anything. We'll first have to remove this wretched ice out of here and I have no idea how long it may take. I can't let these icicles on the books."

"Why not? They are so beautiful. Can't you appreciate their beauty, madam? An ice-trapped library is something special."

"But this is my work, sir! I've handled every one of these books not once but many times. It may be beautiful to you. To me it's a disaster."

Meanwhile, one of the managers turned up yelling at the librarians that none of them would go home until they cleared all the ice off the library, as though it was their fault the plumbers hadn't emptied out the water pipes before the frost. He took the liberty to cut in:

"It would be a pity, sir, to ruin this beautiful work of art that nature has created. It deserves to be photographed and aired on every television channel for the whole world to see. It is a symbol: the freeze that has begun to cripple Romanian research. I'd like to remind you, sir, that I warned you about this as early as last summer."

"You did, didn't you? Well, you look rather pleased it happened after all. Right now, instead of looking on, you'd better give a hand to break this ice."

"Sorry, sir, but I don't have any tools on me except a ballpoint pen, which I don't think will be very effective in this case. Right now there ain't much I can do, but give me a few days and I'll develop a laser-based icebreaking device. Just think of how the ice will sizzle under the plasma jet!"

"No one leaves here until the ice is totally removed," the manager shouted and decamped full speed, trying to avert any further blame-pinning discussion.

He, too, left the scene temporarily, for realizing this was a unique view he dashed to fetch his camera. Unfortunately, by the time he was back, some cleaners that the librarians had called in were senselessly destroying the spectacular scenery. He couldn't take more than a few pictures. Once he had done so, he felt it was his duty to pitch in. Grabbing a pickaxe, he started chipping off the ice cube that stood between him and the book he wanted. The cleaners were complaining about not having any spades. Fortunately, the seismology guys remembered they had some sort of infantry spades at their institute across the yard. Laughter broke out as someone said these were the spades they used to dig up the smaller earthquakes from the ground. A regular merriment erupted. A fellow from a television channel turned up and said he was going to shoot the disaster. He had sneaked in by the doorman hiding the camera somehow, but he didn't stay long. Someone informed the management there was an intruder who wanted to smear the institute on TV. Steps were taken to kick him out immediately:

"Get the fuck out and stay out, or else we smash that camera of yours and you'll have to sell your ass off to repay it."

He went on chopping the ice and every pickaxe blow drew him an inch closer to the desired book. The cleaners muttered they didn't have to do this job, as they hadn't received but scraps of their regular paychecks for the past year or so. The chief librarian screamed at them and their chief yelled at the chief librarian and the ruckus was such that the entire building echoed. Fortunately, some stray reader climbing up to the library slipped on the icy stairs. A thump was heard and everybody rushed to see what happened, but as they reached the stairway, a few more slipped and fell and soon enough there was a heap of squealing bodies on the next landing. The incident had a positive impact, restoring harmony between the wrangling factions that chorused to curse the big boss that was cutting their pay and had reduced them to such indigence they even hadn't enough money to buy salt. Salt had emerged as a pressing necessity, as the ice-covered steps in the dark stairwell had turned into a dangerous trap, taking a considerable toll of broken limbs since the morning. Finally, the chief librarian discovered on a dusty windowsill a jar of salt they'd used for seasoning their lunchtime salads in the summer. Her face suddenly brightened up and she began to sprinkle salt along the corridors and stairs, while her colleagues kept saying that spilling salt was bad omen and she would have an argument with someone.

"Snow, snow, snow," the chief librarian had set off singing while she was scattering the salt around, as though she had gone nuts or something and indeed—whether it was the omen or just another accident—she, too, slipped, broke the jar, and hurt herself.

He had succeeded in digging up a hole into the ice block and taking out the book he wanted, but there were other problems, as water creeping between the pages had frozen so stiff that it wouldn't open. He thought that warming it beneath his coat might help, but a librarian noticed what he was doing and began to yell:

"Shame on you! How can you steal from us when we're in such a mess? We trusted you were a decent man, not one of those that get out with our books beneath their coats. We thought you were here to help."

He tried to make her understand he merely wanted to warm that book, not pinch it, but she wouldn't listen. In fact she probably couldn't even hear him amid the clatter. Swearing without restraint, the cleaners were piling up chops of ice across the corridor into a sort of dam on which everyone stumbled.

He pulled out the book from beneath his coat and said he wanted to check it out, but he only managed to arouse the librarians' anger even worse:

"Who the hell cares about your book right now? Try making yourself useful for a change. Lend a hand, sir, prove yourself a man!"

A person of initiative had brought some trashcans thus turning the discharge of the ice into a systematic operation. Between the shelves, however, the ice layer was still so thick that the pickaxes had an enormous trouble reaching down to the linoleum floor. Lots of ice shards burst out at every blow rising towards the ceiling and falling down into a shower of stars looking like firecrackers. The laser scalpel he had developed years earlier would have been a great help. It could have carved the ice into bars easing the process.

He hadn't given up the idea of borrowing the dripping book, which he was holding tightly in his hand. Once again he tried to open it and cheered out loud when he succeeded. Opening it had been an ill inspired initiative nevertheless: the pages had stuck together growing brittle so they now broke haphazardly. This once again persuaded him of the benefit of writing on clay tablets like they did in Sumer. Paper was much too fragile a material and information was easily lost. He thought he should propose transcribing the entire library on clay tablets that would later be baked and kept on shelves.

"Of course, this is what we should do," he suddenly exclaimed thinking out loud. "Everything we've got here should be inscribed on tablets. We can't go on like this. Every researcher must take a nail and scratch on earthen tiles the book he thinks is most important to him in this library. Then we will bake the tiles and keep them in a safe place. We will be better off this way."

"Have you heard that, folks? Have you heard what the gentleman says should be done at the library?" one of the cleaners who'd overheard him jeered. "God forbid, in a year or two, we might be carrying barrows of tiles and bricks to the laboratories so that the gentlemen researchers may read their articles. You bet they're capable of it."

"Why not, man?" another cleaner joined in. "They might promote us to librarian assistants in this way."

"This is no joke, I mean it," he assured them. "I believe this is the safest way of really storing information in the long term. Stone and ceramic are more resistant than paper or the magnetic support they are advertising so furiously today. As far as I am concerned, I am a fan of the Assyrian tablets that have preserved for us the early human wisdom. I think that in a previous life I must have been a scribe in the great city of Nineveh. I saw a television film on Nineveh the other day and many of the things they showed looked quite familiar to me."

"Man, you sure have one quite loose," a worker said. He'd just got hold of a big mass of ice inside which was a book, and was about to dump it in the trashcan.

"Hey, stop! What are you doing, murderer? Are you dumping a book?" he asked in high astonishment. "Do you realize how much toil and knowledge it takes to make a book?"

"Big deal!" the other retorted with arrogance and contempt A book is nothing but a book and there is plenty of them around."

"Not nearly as many as they should be. Books can never be too many."

"Look, boss, I may be stupid and that's why I work in cleaning, but I'm not nuts. If these books are as important as you say, why the hell have they let the library turn into such mess? A cave, this is what it looks like. Honestly, boss, I'm no one and this is not my business—this is management business—still, things going on up here are sheer mockery. I've never seen anything like this and I believe there can be nothing worse."

"You bet there can," another cleaner, an optimist apparently, replied as he was catching his breath. He had just finished digging with the pickaxe a sort of ditch across the thick ice layer covering the floor. He was wiping the sweat off his face and shaking the white ice slivers off his clothes. He had warmed up and seemed quite excited about his work: "Now, if I had a crowbar, I could loosen this ice pack that has caught the chief's chair and open up a way to that shelf over there."

"Cool down, man," one of his fellows tried to quiet him. "Wait till next summer when the sun is up and it will all melt by itself."

"Stop horsing around and get down to work! Look, there's an inspection coming."

"Hi, boys!"

"Hello, Uncle Gica! I almost failed to recognize you. You've rounded out some, I'd say. But I expect anyone would with your cushy job: no trouble, fat pay, dainty delegations—"

"Well, boys, I too did some apprenticeship in my day. When I was your age, all of them bosses, especially the chairman, used to ride roughshod over me. You're young; you never knew the chairman."

"Yeah, sure, but now you're snug. Driving here and there like a big shot."

"I've dropped by to see this mess. Looks more like Scarisoara Cave than like a library. If old man Hulubei rose from the dead and saw what has become of his work, I think he'd hang the current bosses with his own bare hands."

"Hang them? What for? Can't you see, Uncle Gica, it's the same thing everywhere? As Mayor Basescu said, 'winter is not like summer'."

"Right. Nor is onion like roast. Nowadays the main thing is to manage. Things are no longer what they used to be. In the old days, one could still go fishing on the pond after work, or play backgammon in the yard with neighbors. Now, you've got to be on the move around the clock, seize opportunities. The chief librarian, for example, if she had any business sense in her, she would sell tickets for this view. Look at these charming stalactites and stalagmites! We even have speleologists among us already. Look at this gentleman researcher how keenly he examines that ice lump as though he has discovered some prehistoric bug inside—"

It was he that the visitor meant and he loathed being mocked like that. He had to put the man in his place.

"Look, Mr. Gica," he said trying to keep his temper, "I won't be mocked by you, or by anyone else for that matter. I'm a researcher and will be treated with all due respect. I won't allow you to scoff at me the way you used to do back when you were the chairman's driver. The times have changed indeed. Right now I'm trying to save a capital book these boys were about to discard as trash. It's trapped in this wretched ice boulder. I keep thinking how to set it free without spoiling it, while you are scoffing. I don't like it at all."

"Sir, I apologize, you see, I didn't know. Please pardon me. I do respect researchers, but it's the way I am, I mean, I sometimes put my foot in my mouth—"

As the man continued to eat crow, he raised the boulder and held it out under the driver's eyes.

"Have you any idea what book lies here under ice? Can you see what the cover says? Take a good look: it's J. J. Thomson! Do you know who J. J. Thomson was?" Then he burst out furiously: "Gentlemen! What's happening here is a crime! A library is a treasury in which the values of mankind are kept. Writings endure for centuries. What's going on here is inadmissible! In-ad-mis-si-ble!"

He woke up yelling wildly in the dark. There was no one around. Isaac the cat, his friend, had set out on a ramble around the tower and his faint mews came back at times amid the howls of wind.

He suddenly felt frightened remembering the order he had been given in the wilderness. He was a careless jerk and a nuisance to everyone around him. He'd rushed the wise Nabir and his whole caravan to set out in the middle of the night, then instead of riding to Nineveh with him, he sneaked back like a coward to the library in Tower B to dig up books from ice and squabble with managers, drivers, and cleaners.

As to Nabir, he should have told the wise man straight that he, as a researcher, was much more interested in the tablets than in the fate of Nineveh, but it was now too late. Nabir was far by now; his caravan had probably arrived in the great city, while he stayed behind in that dark tower where he was freezing so badly that his teeth had started to chatter. The darkness that surrounded him was growing thicker. An open window was banging in the wind, rattling his brains. The tomcat's mews could no longer be heard. Even his good friend Isaac had deserted him, chilled to the bone perhaps and searching for a warmer shelter in some lost corners of the tower maze he was the only one to know.

* * *

Not little was his joy as he once again found himself riding alongside Nabir ahead of the file of laden camels. The caravan had stopped before a grandiose gate overlooked by a high, bulwarked tower. Wearied by their wake, the sentinels were dozing on their spears, while the city roosters were heralding the luminary of the day that was rising just then, blenching the horizon beyond the massive walls of the city. Catching sight of the wise Nabir leading the caravan, the gatekeepers were quick to open and greet him with most chosen words.

"Welcome home, wise Nabir! May the morning star protect you! The city will be filled with joy today learning the wisest of its wise men is back."

Nabir nodded and put his right hand on his chest in response, then took out a few coins from his purse and handed them to the chief of the guards.

Arriving on the square outside the Rulers' Palace, the caravan stopped off at the Lions' Pool, also known as the Seven Lions' Fountain for the number of its stone-carved lion heads, the seven mouths of which gushed forth drinking water carried by an earthen pipe from the River Khusur. As Nabir clapped his hands three times, his camel kneeled, and he got down, wiped the road dust off his clothes, and went to cool his face right from the third font, as the third lion was the protector of the city's wise men. He bade his companion to do the same, but the other contented himself with water from the pool, like common people did, drinking a few gulps to quench his thirst, and pouring the rest on his head to freshen up.

"Why do you bend over the pool like common people rather than drink right from the clear spring that flows out of the lions' mouths? You are my guest and I will do my best to honor you as such and see that the city people bow at your feet and obey you as the savior you are."

"Oh, wise Nabir! I have not come to Nineveh to receive praise and honors. I have been sent here on a mission with a definite order to carry out. If you wish your city well and want to reward me for my trouble, please convene as shortly as possible the rulers and the wise men of the city so that I may inform them of the end that is to come."

"There is a time for everything, my righteous friend. First, it is meet that we should stop under my roof, catch our breath, break bread, and rejoice for the good ending of our journey."

"The days of Nineveh are counted, wise man, and every moment draws the city closer to its ruin."

But Nabir hushed him, as the servants had joined them at the fountain to drink and wash their faces. Among them were some Ninevites, out on some early morning business in the city, who were inquiring about the goods the caravan had brought back from its journey, and spying on their conversations. The stranger that accompanied the caravan probably aroused some curiosity as well and many wondered why a city elder like Nabir was mixing with a shabby stranger and even treated him with such ceremonies.

One of the servants went home ahead of the rest to announce the arrival of the master and indeed, when they entered the courtyard, the entire household was astir and they were met with honors according to the customs.

The servants fetched clean garments and Nabir took a hot bath in a rock scoop near his bedroom. Two slaves carried in expensive balms and anointed his body and then the master rested for a while under a canopy enjoying the fresh morning air.

He had meanwhile retired in a corner of the courtyard bewildered by a strange thing that was happening to him. It had all started as he washed his face at the Lions' Pool in the early morning. Since then, his eyes had opened up and he could see through people and walls. He also felt ill at ease in the prison of his own body and was tempted to slip out of it and be free. He could see and hear things that were happening far away and all he had to do was think of them.

The beauty and greatness of Nineveh overwhelmed him, yet terrible sins were being committed inside her walls—sins that filled him with fright now that he was able to watch them taking place all over the city. He was beginning to feel sorry that all of these proud towers, strong walls, and shining palaces would be razed, as the voice said they would when it had spoken to him in the wilderness. Right now, he had to admit such retribution appeared inevitable and their attempt—Nabir's and his— to save the city seemed most unlikely to succeed. This made him grow increasingly concerned about the tablets.

As he was pondering these grim thoughts, he saw a hut beneath a withered vine. In it there lived a man full of years who spoke to him:

"Researcher, you are keen on saving the king's tablets, yet don't you think you'd better try to act in such a way that Nineveh itself be spared and everything in her be left untouched?"

"Nothing would give me greater joy, wise man. I would be happy if not a single stone fell from her walls and everything stayed as is, but what I see is happening in this city has made my blood run cold. The Ninevites are so extremely wicked and indulge in such horrendous sins that I'm afraid God's wrath will soon be upon them."

"There is one way," the old man said. "Urge the Ninevites to repent. Go to their rulers and tell them to mend their evil ways and repent of their sins with all their hearts and spirits. I did so myself and I succeeded, although I disobeyed at first and shied away, and put off carrying out my mission. I ran away at sea and hid below deck but the Lord's anger caught up with me, and a violent storm arose. Then lots were cast and it turned out I was responsible for that calamity, so I myself asked to be thrown into the sea, but the Lord provided a great fish and commanded it to swallow me and bring me back to shore so that I could at last fulfill His will. I came to Nineveh and urged and pleaded so strongly and so ardently that its inhabitants repented and the city did not perish. I was successful, now you try!"

Hearing the old man's story, he realized who had spoken to him and shivered. When the slaves came to him fetching fresh clothes and bidding him to bathe and cleanse his body, he thanked them for their trouble and said he needed nothing but a handful of ashes, which as they presently provided, he spread onto his head and clothes. Dumbfounded, the slaves promptly reported to their master that his guest was a weird man that spurned the privilege of washing his body at the bath and putting on clean garments.

The wise Nabir girded his robe, put on a pair of chamois sandals, and went out to the yard. He found his guest sitting on a stone in a shaded corner where the dogs usually sought refuge from the heat.

"Righteous researcher, you ought to do me the honor of sharing my recreations," the host told him reproachfully. "Why should you put ashes on your head while you enjoy my hospitality?"

"Wise Nabir, please be assured I mean no disrespect, nor do I wish to trouble the joy you rightly feel for being back among your loved ones. My spirit nonetheless is in too great a pain that I might share any of it. Ever since I drank the water of the Lions' Pool, my eyes have opened and seen such frightening things that I am even afraid to mention them, let alone describe them to anyone alive."

"Tell me, my friend," Nabir asked warily, "what was it that you saw under my roof that may have so appalled you and prompted you to seek the company of dogs in this retired place?" But his guest shunned the question:

"I cannot tell you, wise man. My words would anger you too much and prompt you to rash acts. Lay this matter to rest for now and hurry to gather the leaders of this city, as you promised, for I must talk to them."

"I'll do exactly as I planned," Nabir replied fighting back a growing apprehension. "I will throw a big party to celebrate my return and ask every prominent man in the city, as wine, choice food, and pretty dancers are the only arguments that can bring them together."

"Oh, it won't work. Do you believe the leaders of this city, with bellies full, minds blurred by wine, and lusty eyes on swinging bodies, will pay any attention to my words? Much rather ask a servant to open up our way blowing a trumpet and let's go back to the Lions' Pool. There, on the central square, we'll gather all the Ninevites and urge them to repent. Take my example, put ashes on your head: the time of penitence has come."

Nabir gave him a bewildered glance. The hot bath had relaxed his mind and body. The balms the slaves had lavished on his limbs made him feel lighter than a bird, and the cool clean robe he was wearing put him at ease.

"My righteous friend," he said halfheartedly, "I would most resolutely embrace your plan if I thought such public exhortations to repentance were of use, but, trust me, I know the Ninevites. They're stubborn people that listen to no one except their rulers and wise men and only if they think what they are asked to do is in accordance with their ancient laws and customs. If we take to the streets with drums and bugles to rally them in the central square, they will undoubtedly believe we've lost our minds and stone us to death."

Looking at his host with sympathy, he sighed:

"I understand your misgivings, wise man. You are a prominent person in Nineveh and cannot possibly appear on the central square alongside me, a shabby researcher coming to a rich city and urging her to give up her evil ways. So I'll go it alone, or else, believe me, Nineveh will soon be overturned."

The wise Nabir realized all too well there was no way to stop his steadfast, single-minded guest. Still he remembered they had made a pact the other night and felt ashamed to be backing down like this.

"Do as you wish. Go through the city, tell them what you know, warn them of their destruction. My home will be open for you whenever you grow weary and my table will be there for you when you are hungry."

He rose to his feet, collected his knotty staff and patchy bag, and took his leave, thanking the wise Nabir for his fine hospitality and blessing the home and fortune of the man that had brought him to Nineveh.

The sun had risen above the city and was beginning to warm up the slabs his bare feet were treading with determination en route to the Lions' Pool. People stared at him along the way, particularly as he stopped at crossroads, struck the pavement with his staff, and cried out as loud as he could: "People of Nineveh, come to the big square to hear the prophecy against your city!"

Many a passer-by went after him out of curiosity. Merchants let servants look after the trade and followed him. Slaves strayed from their errands to join the growing crowd that accompanied him to the square. He knew many of these people considered him some sort of lunatic, but didn't care any longer.

Once he had reached the square, he headed straight for the Rulers Palace, skimmed boldly by the guards that watched over the entrance, stopped before the heavy copper-paneled cedar gate, and started knocking with his staff and shouting:

"Rulers of Nineveh! You who trample the law instead of maintaining justice in the courts! You who cram the city's riches into your bags and barrels instead of looking after her prosperity! Come out and listen to the prophecy!"

The noisy babbling crowd that had been scoffing him for putting ashes on his head was stunned to see him knock at the palace gate at which they didn't even dare to gaze too long for fear of the guards. Silently, they backed off and some even began to run away along the streets, for they all knew what was next: whenever an uprising broke out and rioters converged on the palace, the rulers would send out the mounted spearmen and rivers of blood would be shed on the square.

Indeed several soldiers rushed to grab him, but he cried out raising his staff against them:

"The curse be on your people till the end of time if you dare touch me! Stop serving wicked masters and repent!"

Miraculously, the soldiers froze in awe, dropped their weapons, and fell on their knees, begging for pardon. Their conduct emboldened him to restart pounding on the gate and shouting:

"Repent, or else your city will be overturned! The end is near!"

The noisy commotion that was taking place outside drew the attention of Haiff himself, the Great Ruler, who showed up on an upper terrace of the palace. As from up there he couldn't make out what was going on, he sent out a spy to take a look.

The servant sneaked out through a side door and hung around a bit. His face was white with fear when he returned to his master. He reported that a shabby stranger had just climbed on the pedestal where the next king's statue was to be erected and stood there shouting terrible things which he said would happen to the city.

"He says all of us will perish by fire unless we repent. And that the walls of the city will crumble into dust and no one will even know where Nineveh once stood."

"Some madman. The sun of the desert must have broiled his mind," the Great Ruler said scornfully. "What are the guards doing down there? He should have been nabbed, flogged, and jailed by now. What are they waiting for?"

"Noble master, the guards—" the spy stammered and humbly bowed his head. "The guards have fallen on their knees before him. They do not dare lay hands on him."

"What are you talking about?" the great Haiff snarled furiously. Send out the spearmen to throw him into prison right away."

"Master, it was the wise Nabir that brought him into town at dawn today. Rumors have it Nabir has read the stars and found this man will save the city from destruction, the same as the prophet Yunus did in the ancient days when he came to Nineveh and urged our forefathers to change their ways."

The news that Nabir had brought along the rabble-rouser came as a shock to Haiff. His face turned red with anger, as he set out striding back and forth across the rulers' council hall, crying like mad:

"Nabir, of course, I should have figured. It is his hand all over. He's dying to unsaddle me and grab the throne, deprive me of my lawful right. Put that raving lunatic into irons. This will cool his broiled mind and teach him to leave my city alone!"

As soon as ordered, Ritti, son of Karal,, chief commander of the spearmen, sent a few soldiers to run in the prophet. He knew they were coming, as he could see inside the palace, but did not flinch. Up on the plinth, he continued to preach repentance to the crowd that had flocked back to listen to him.

He was still speaking when the soldiers' nooses caught him by the neck and brought him down while the fearful crowd were scattering as quickly as they could. He didn't resist and let himself be dragged across the square and into the jail, a dark cellar where they put him into chains. He didn't really care, knowing that, while the body stayed behind in fetters, his mind would still be free to travel as far as he wanted.

He wondered what was going on at Nabir's place and saw the wise man surrounded by people, friends and strangers, that had come by to tell him the prophet he had brought along from the wilderness had been arrested. Nabir felt sorry for leaving the researcher on his own and hurried to the palace to see Haiff.

"Peace to you, Great Ruler!" he said and bowed according to the custom. "The stranger you have thrown into prison is a righteous researcher and an honest prophet. I fear that wronging him might elicit some punishment against the city. Pray order that he be presently released. He bears the signs I've read about in the stars. He is assigned to urge us to repentance and protect us against the evil that is looming upon us."

Barely containing his rage, Haiff made an impatient gesture meaning this was out of the question, but the wise man pressed on:

"Great Ruler, it has happened before: You know about the prophet Yunus who in the ancient times saved Nineveh from imminent disaster. The then king listened to him, covered himself with sackcloth, and sat down in the dust and so did the entire people. Like Nebi Yunus, this new prophet has come to warn us that our evil deeds have multiplied beyond all limits and our wickedness has once again sullied the city."

"Oh, cunning stargazer," Haiff cut in violently, "how do you dare approach me with your smooth-tongued stories? How do you dare pick madmen from the wilderness and display them as prophets in my city? I've been told ugly things about you and I've known for quite a while that you were waiting and conspiring to take my place and later on become the king of Nineveh."

Shaken by the allegations, the wise man tore the garments on his chest and said in dismay:

"What reckless spies told you these lies, Great Ruler? How can you even conceive such things? How can you think I'm coveting your seat? My wealth is large enough for me and I don't desire anything that is not mine."

Haiff, however, did not content himself with this response, but called in witnesses and made the wise man swear in their presence that he did not hanker for the Great Ruler's office and would never plot to overturn him.

Pondering what Nabir had said about the stranger that was now in irons and learning that groups of armed men were gathering around the city to demand the prophet's release, Haiff began to fear an uprising. He decided the best thing he could do was to convene a meeting of the rulers and envoys were presently dispatched around the town to every one of those great men.

*   *   *

When the time came, they brought him fettered before the rulers' assembly. They quizzed and taunted him in many ways, but he didn't answer. He just kept silent for a while, gazing at each and every one of them. Then, even though he was in chains and covered with injuries and bruises, as the jailers had dragged and hit him all the way across the palace court, he boldly, forcefully confronted them.

"Oh you, who rule this city, open your eyes and see the mischief that takes place under your authority. Lend your ears to the wails of the wronged and quickly turn to the path of justice, otherwise the city's end is near."

"How do you dare berate us, crazy stranger?" the head of the grain merchants' guild snapped at him. "How can you talk to us like that without knowing who we are or how we strive to feed the people of this city down to the very poorest of them? Do you have any idea how many good deeds we have done, how many times we have saved the residents of this city from starvation?"

"I only know what I am shown," he said staring at the grain merchant as though his face was some sort of a book. "Right now I am looking at you and seeing things that this assembly doesn't know about you."

"Oh, really? Pray tell us what you see," the merchant scoffed.

He did not answer at once. He looked intently at the ruler for a few moments, then started speaking softly:

"I see a file of camels carrying away heavy loads of grain smuggled from the city granaries to be sold to foreign peoples beyond Mesopotamia. I see you stash the gold thus earned into an earthen pot, which you have buried beneath the threshold of your house."

The merchant suddenly turned very pale. His beard was sweating and began to shake. The council members exchanged astonished glances, but no one said anything except the head of the oil and spice merchants. Rising from his seat, he countered:

"How does a deranged man like you dare to appear before this assembly and slander the most honorable Bubu, who feeds the widows and orphans and gives charity to the needy? Your visions are designed to divide us and jeopardize the peace of our city. If you are doing it by yourself, then what you do is wrong. And if some spirit is prompting you to act this way, it's a deceitful spirit."

He looked at the speaker as long and intently as he had stared at Bubu, then said in the same low voice as before:

"I apologize to this assembly if my words are disturbing any one of you, but I think you had better know the man that has just challenged me is as unworthy of his office as the one that spoke before him. Several years ago, I see him return with his master from the city of Nippur where they had made good profit selling oil and spice. I see them stopping on the way and I see this man stab his master and leave his body to the beasts of prey. And afterwards I see him enter with his bags of gold into a great city that has a fountain with seven lion heads, and rise through bribery and artfulness to become a ruler of this city."

On hearing this, the spice merchant flew into a rage. His hand felt for the ivory hilted dagger strapped at his belt and he would have stabbed his accuser right there before his peers if the Great Ruler had not ordered the guards to defend the prisoner.

"Tell us, stranger: is there anyone sitting in this room worthy of his office?" asked Tamir, the High Priest, who had noticed the council members all looked extremely worry as though big secret sins burdened their hearts.

"I'm telling you the truth: no one in here deserves the high position that he holds."

"What then are we supposed to do? Shall we step down and leave the city to itself? Shall we give up collecting taxes or enforcing the laws and regulations of this city?"

"Not at all," he replied. "All you must do is mend your wicked ways, confess your sins before the people, put ashes on your head, and live in penitence from now on."

All heads were now turned towards the High Priest that remained silent in his seat, patting his beard and gazing at the ragged stranger, who flanked by spearmen was silent as well. The Great Ruler himself was just as worried as everybody else and didn't dare say anything lest the stranger should start disclosing certain facts in his own past, since he apparently could read on a man's face as in an open book.

The stranger noticed that everyone was waiting for the High Priest to speak and said:

"The High Priest can't be of any use or comfort to you. He too has sinned considerably, only I am forbidden to reveal his sins, because his name is written in the Book of Peoples and must not be soiled."

"How can we have our own names inscribed in that book?" one of the council members asked cunningly.

"This is completely out of reach to common people and very hard to achieve to great men, since a man's deeds are quite thoroughly weighed and only those who turn out worthy are inscribed. Their names will thereby be preserved for centuries and ages in testimony of their faith and virtue."

Once he had said that, the conference room became so quiet that one could hear the voices of the crowd that had gathered again outside the palace on the Lions' Fountain

Square. Eventually breaking the silence, the wise Nabir asked for permission to speak.

"Brothers," he said, "as I was coming home from my journey the other night, I left the servants take care of the camp and climbed up a hill to examine the skies. As usual, my eyes first searched for the Great Bear, the stars of which have always been known to govern the fate of Nineveh. It saddened me to see the stars presaged great dangers and adversities, but at the same time I was relieved to find there was a way out. The stars showed me that the redeemer of our city was quite close and indeed, when I climbed down the hill, there he was in my own camp tied to a camel's neck, as my servants suspected him to be the robber that had plundered our caravan earlier on our way. I set him free, apologized, and brought him into town, offering him the hospitality of my own home. And now I see this very man, a prophet, fettered and under heavy guard, as if he were a dangerous criminal of some sort. He has been sent to guide us on the right path, as Nebi Yunus did in the old times, and we have thrown this man in prison, instead of showing him our full submission and gratitude. Are we right to do so?"

"Certainly not. We must release him presently and listen to his teachings," said several members of the council.

"We will discuss this right away," said the Great Ruler, ordering the spearmen to take the prisoner back to his cell. Then, on his bidding, the council moved to a secluded room where capital decisions were usually taken far from the servants' ears. Once they had checked that there was no intruder in the room, they locked the door and Great Ruler Haiff began to speak in a lamenting voice:

"Woe is us, brothers! Woe is us, for our sins are coming back to haunt us. This man appears indeed to be a prophet, as he can see through the darkest secrets of our lives. If the people of Nineveh that are now waiting outside the palace happen to uncover our sins, a great confusion will arise and no one will obey us any longer. We must get rid of this prophet as quickly as we can and make sure the Ninevites never see or hear him again."

"I suggest we drown him in the river as soon as tonight," said Bubu, the chief of the grain merchants. "I'll hire two guards to tie a boulder to his neck and throw him into the Tigris."

"I think we'd better take him out of the city after sunset and leave him tied up in the Lions Vale. The beasts will eat him up by morning and we won't have his blood falling upon us," said another councilman.

"What if he gets away somehow and we have him on our backs all over again?" said the oil and spice merchant. "I say we'd better kill him and bury him secretly right here, in some remote dungeon of the palace. There will be no trace of him left in this way."

"How can you even consider such horrors?" the wise Nabir berated them. "Are you not afraid of sin? Don't you see that his blood will fall upon our households and the entire city? I propose that we heed his warning and repent, and urge the people to take our example. The city won't be saved unless we do so."

"Look, stargazer," snarled the Great Ruler, "if you feel like putting ashes on your head and pummeling your own chest at crossroads, and reciting your sins to every lowlife, then you are free to do so. I think such conduct would be completely out-of-date and ill advised. We'd be better off continuing to run the city without confessing to the scum."

Then Tamir raised his voice asking for silence.

"Honorable rulers," said the High Priest, "I've thought it over and found a solution, which though not to our liking can restore peace and quiet to Nineveh. I see no other way. As far as I can tell, the man Nabir has brought here from the wilderness is a true prophet. I haven't grasped so far wherefrom he's got these powers that show him the lives and sins of others, but I intend to clear this out. The Ninevites already hold him to be a seer and you all know how much they value people of this kind. Can you imagine the unrest, the riots that will break out if we expel or kill this man? In the circumstances, the wisest thing for us to do is to co-opt him, name him a member of our council. I'm positive that he will shortly become like everybody else caught in the mire of human sins from which there is no escape. Greed and lust will shortly overwhelm him, his seeing powers will be dimmed, his popular support will ebb away, and finally he'll either realize his own decay and go away, or we will throw him out like a bad tooth and go ahead with our businesses in peace."

The High Priest's words made quite an impression on the councilmen who indeed agreed to it after a brief reflection. From then on, they decided Nineveh would have one more official that would be responsible for checking the residents' sins and inscribing them on clay tablets. Haiff did not believe the High Priest's solution was going to work. He didn't think public peace would easily be restored. Besides, he hated the prospect of eating humble pie. He felt his topmost office was in danger. Losing the highest post meant all the fortune he'd spent on buying it would be thrown out the window. Struggling to refrain his misgivings, the Great Ruler commanded the stranger should be set free. He also ordered garments should be provided him to match his current dignity as an official of the city.

"Don't bother about that. He won't accept them anyway and will keep wearing his old rags," said the wise Nabir. "This prophet sets no store on clothes. Back at my place, the servants offered him a clean robe, but he turned it down and instead asked for ashes that he spread on his head."

"Ashes? Fine, then we'll supply him all the ashes he needs," Haiff said mockingly.

"I'm afraid we'll need some ashes too, to prove our contrition," said the High Priest. "Send out the servants to the blacksmiths to fetch as much as they can find. We will put ashes on our heads and go out before the people and show everyone we are deeply sorry for our past wickedness."

6

WHEN THE TIME CAME, THEY PULLED him out of jail and took him before the assembly once again. There they were, all of them, including the High Priest, with their precious garments torn and ashes spread on their heads. He didn't seem surprised.

"Oh, prominent men of Nineveh, joy is your deed if penitence has stamped out vanity within your spirits. If you are doing it with all your hearts, this city will rejoice, as from now on it will see pride come down and humility rise; it will see riches and poverty wiping out the border that divides them, truth crushing lies, and justice replacing iniquity."

"Let it be so!" the rulers chorused, while he resolutely rushed to the ash pot the servants had fetched in and filled his hands with yet more ashes he scattered on his head and clothes.

"Ashes," he said. "We need more ashes! It's time for us to come out of the palace and call on the entire people to repent."

With Haiff and the High Priest leading the file, they walked out of the palace and headed for the Lions' Pool, while the astonished crowd that packed the square could not believe their eyes. The stranger holding his patchy bag and knotty staff came behind them crying out loud, urging repentance. The palace guards had formed two rows, one on each side of the big gate. Their heads were lowered and every trace of pride seemed to have vanished from their faces. On top of the pedestal a drummer was beating furiously his drum calling all inhabitants to the square. When the Great Ruler held up his arm asking for silence, everyone instantly shut up and for several moments the sound of water purling out from the stone lions' mouths was heard alone. Then Tamir, the High Priest, rose his arms to the skies and thundered:

"Ninevites, the time has come to repent! We all have soiled the city with our sins and now disaster is looming upon us. A messenger has been sent to guide us to repentance and I'm asking all of you to obey him. He will sit here on the square day in, day out, and see that every sin that you confess out loud, with due contrition, is inscribed on tablets. Ashes will be provided so that there be enough for all to put some on your heads and clothes, to mark your repentance. Do as this prophet tells you, as we, your rulers, have decided that he be one of us starting today. His office will be a new one, unheard of so far, and will consist in keeping records of the sins and wrongdoings we confess. Written on tablets, they will remain as proof of our repentance. Do as he tells you, knowing that your confession and contrition are the only way to save the city. Don't be afraid or shy away from telling your wicked deeds."

As the Great Ruler hailed, the servants who were waiting at the palace gates fetched in two ewers full of ashes, while the scribes were preparing tablets to start writing down everyone's sins. The council members filed past the ewers first. Putting some ashes on his head, every one of them said in a humble voice, but loud enough so that the crowd could hear him, "I have wronged and abused. I'm begging for forgiveness." The scribes wrote these words on a tablet and every ruler put his stamp beneath to further show he unambiguously subscribed to that avowal. Taking his mission seriously, the stranger supervised the process, while the crowd looked on in disbelief. As the last ruler on the file completed his confession, the High Priest turned to them:

"Up to you now, people of Nineveh! Put ashes on your heads and confess whatever is on your consciences. Do so with full determination, for there's no other way to redeem the city from disaster."

The drum rolled once again, the sentinels sounded the trumpets on the city walls, and the rulers returned into the palace followed by the guard. He stayed behind by the pool among the scribes urging the common people to come up and make a clean breast of their sins. Yet what he saw was going on inside the palace saddened his heart.

Great Ruler Haiff had ordered that the gates be firmly locked. No servant was to leave the palace any more; no rumor from inside would be allowed to leak beyond the walls. The big pool in the summer wing had been prepared and slaves were waiting there with fresh clothes, wine, and ointments. The council members bathed at length, washed every trace of ashes off their bodies, put on rich garments, and went to party and make merry on a terrace facing the Tigris, far from the bustle of the crowd that still confessed their sins and scattered ashes on their heads. Musicians and dancers were called in, wine was poured, and trays with delicatessen filled the tables. Toasting to the health of them all, the High Priest said:

"Finally, brothers, this incident has turned to our advantage: Thinking that we have changed for real, the crowd will become more respectful. That nuts coming from nowhere will go on pressing them to repent, so they won't even want to riot for a while. But our greatest profit will consist of knowing everything about our people. The tablets will preserve their testimonies and from now on provide us countless excuses to throw them into prison whenever we like."

"Your advice has been a wise and valuable one, High Priest," Haiff acknowledged. A threat looming on us and Nineveh has indeed turned to our benefit. Let's cheer and drink to this for we carried the day."

On his signal, the musicians started to play and the dancers picked their tambourines and began to sway their bodies jingling the strings of beads and little bells they wore around their necks and hips. With eyes made misty by the strong wine, the rulers of Nineveh watched the young dancers and enjoyed their party.

* * *

Outside the palace, the Ninevites were still queuing before the ash pots and the scribes who wrote down their names and sins on tablets. Those who were going home and met some passer-by that didn't yet have ashes in his hair urged him to hurry to the square, confess and take the ashes of penitence. More and more residents turned out so that the lines before the scribes seemed to be growing rather than thinning. Back on the pedestal from which the guards had dragged him down that morning, he kept the crowd in order, chided them when any trouble occurred, and never tired of preaching full and complete repentance.

The sun was going down and the shadows of the city towers fell upon the square cooling the slabs after the day's heat. Despite the great numbers of people, the place was almost quiet. Those who were still waiting for their turn spoke mostly in a low voice and the earlier din had turned into a drone. At that particular moment, a palace servant appeared shouting at the top of his lungs. Sickened by the debauchery that was taking place inside, the man had managed to sneak out and was breaking the news to the crowd:

"The rulers have deceived you: they have not repented. They've washed the ashes off their bodies, put on fresh clothes, and right now they're dead drunk banging the slaves. So much for the contrition of these sons of whores! Woe is Nineveh! The city will be destroyed because of them."

The news that their leaders had betrayed them shocked the people. Their surprise, however, quickly gave way to anger. While the square was filling with clamor once again, some of the men, though furious, decided they'd better seek the prophet's advice before taking any action.

"Righteous man, don't you think we should waste those bastards? A short while ago they were still here weeping and pressing us to repent and now they're drinking and whoring shamelessly. They're simply making fools of us. Shall we just let that happen? You're an official of the city now: we will obey you; everyone will. Command and we will follow. Take control of the palace! Order us to march on it! We want you to be the leader of our city. We think this way it will be spared and no catastrophe will fall on us or our children.

"Your hearts are pure, men of Nineveh," he answered. "You're right that these double-dealers should not be allowed to rule the city any longer. They must no longer be obeyed, nor have the power to impose obedience."

"Give us an order and you'll see how it is carried out. Let's put these traitors to the sword."

"You will not want to take upon yourselves another sin, will you?" he tried to calm them down. "Besides, they don't need to be killed: living in sin is to be dead already. And being dead, they're no concern of ours any longer. Let them wallow in lust and recklessness, while we will focus on the living. If you are really determined to take my advice, you can change many things to the better."

"We will take your advice, righteous man," they answered. "Tell us what we have to do."

"First of all, I want you to help me hammer out new laws for Nineveh. The old ones were not good enough, as they neither kept you from wicked deeds, nor prompted you to kindness to your neighbors or the fallen. Humility and self-restraint will guide you from now on."

The men appeared extremely happy to hear him talk like this. They lifted him on their arms and carried him around the fountain shouting: "Here is our leader that will make us new laws! We will obey no one but him. Our old rulers are dead. They don't exist to us no longer."

The crowd gathered around them. Many cheered the plan of putting down new laws and acclaimed the legislator. Some of the scribes instead were frightened and ran away, leaving behind their tablets that were trampled by the crowd. By contrast, the palace guards, disgusted with their masters' conduct, hailed the new laws and sided with the crowd.

The sun had sunk painting in red the dunes that bordered the horizon on the other bank of the Tigris. Increasingly more people were gathering around the Lions' Pool to find out more about the new laws. Torches had been lit and a few men turned up with some old cedar beams and built a bonfire to make sure there would be enough light where the new laws were going to be born. Meanwhile, he had climbed back on the plinth that was designed to hold the statue of the new king and from up there he made a fiery speech:

"Men of Nineveh, who have to toil and sweat to make a living, the time has come for you to shake the burden of your past sins off your hearts and engage on the path of justice. You, who know all too well how evil is committed, be ready to mend your ways and stop harming your neighbors. I've come all the way to Nineveh to tell you these things and urge you to repentance. Unless you make amends, the wicked deeds that are constantly done within your walls will be the end of you and your city. To keep the proper laws and order, each of your tribes will have to elect a worthy man, to represent them. The men you will elect will replace your former rulers that have perished forever from our midst, killed by the sins that overpowered their minds." As soon as he finished his speech, he asked the scribes that sided with the people to prepare tablets for the new code of the city and waited for the tribes to make their choices.

After a brief deliberation under the flambeaus, the Ninevites sent forward seven men, one each for the tribes living in the city. Having the blessing of their kin, they came to join him by the bonfire that burnt near the Lions' Pool, while the rest of the crowd backed off to leave their representatives ponder the city's needs in peace and bring out good new laws.

*　　*　　*

At break of day, the rulers were still reveling, but he could see the wise Nabir, the only one of them who was still sober, slipping out of the palace through a secret door and hurrying back home, where he locked himself up in a room and sighing frequently remembered every moment of the previous day and felt devastated by remorse.

The scribes had worked all night filling numerous tablets with the new laws the seer and the seven Ninevites were churning out guided by their honest hearts and spirits. On the outskirts of the city, the stonecutters that were in charge of the furnaces were wasting no time. Heating the hearths, they started baking the new tables to make sure they would endure.

Meanwhile, on the big square, the small council was busy devising more and more provisions for the city's good, but the crowd that had loitered away the night around them were growing tired of waiting. As they were beginning to grumble, the lawmakers decided to convene a broad assembly of the people and have the legislation read out to them. On the square, many were critical already, as they had learned from hearsay that the new laws were to punish hard drinking, whoring, and sodomy on a par with thievery and murder. The owners of the city's thriving brothels were scared to death and started to egg on the people to rush and stone out of the square the self-styled legislators who were desecrating the old canon and forcing unheard of, tougher, rules on Nineveh.

"Isn't it right that all men growing fed up with their women find solace in our houses of delight and when they leave feel happier, rejuvenated, and full of renewed energy to the great profit of the city? Why should we close these houses that are a benefit to all? And what would then become of the fine, lovely creatures we have taken such trouble to bring to Nineveh for your enjoyment? These self-appointed rulers have no right to deprive you of your little pleasures. Come, let's drive them out!"

The merchants, too, were worried. Rumors had it that those who tampered with their scales and weights would be thrown behind bars or forced to hugely compensate the deceived. No sooner had they opened up their stores than they closed down and stowed away their goods to avoid seizure, looting or whatever could befall in troubled times like those. Besides, they knew that common people faced with scarcity could easily be turned against the new rules.

"If we all agree to stop selling anything as of today and hide away our goods, the city will shortly be so starved that the new rulers will fall down on their knees before us and grant us anything we like lest they be stoned to death by hungry mobs."

The city's thieves, who stalked the merchants and everyone that couldn't or wouldn't take good care of their property, were similarly upset by the new rules, which they feared could cause them lots of trouble, including endless terms in jail.

Only the beggars, who had like brothers divided amongst themselves the city's crossroads where they asked for alms, were pleased to hear that the new rules made charity a mandatory duty of every citizen. They, too, however were concerned about a rumor that they'd be rounded up and forced to work in exchange for food and lodging, a frightening prospect, since no one had ever heard of beggars doing any work.

The public reading of the laws upset a lot of Ninevites who left the square spitting and cursing or at least nursing plans of vengeance and rebellion. By noon few people remained around the Lions' Pool under the scorching sun. Many had gone home hungry and tired and disappointed, or just retired in the neighborhood in search of shade around the trees and buildings.

Along with a few members of his panel, he had stayed beside the fountain. Yet weary himself after his long watch, he finally rested his head on his old bag and lied down at the foot of a wall to get some sleep. His conduct made many eyebrows rise: it was quite unbecoming for the new ruler of the city to lie down on the ground like beggars instead of resting in the big palace that now was his by right. He was aware of their critiques, but wanted no greatness for himself and feared that the mere proximity of riches would taint his body and soul. He had to bear nevertheless that two armed guards watch over him during his sleep just in case anyone would try to harm him in some way.

*　　*　　*

The rulers' party didn't end till morning. A detail of spearmen stopped them when they tried to walk out the gate and go home. They were not allowed to leave the palace, the soldiers told them. At first, they couldn't believe the guards were mutinying. A spy they sent to snoop around the square made an even more incredible report: they were considered dead. The astounding news sobered them up at once. They held a meeting and decided to restore order in the city and have their own rights restored as well. They first sent for Ritti, son of Karal,. Since many of his spearmen had rebelled, the guard commander was so frightened that he took refuge in a palace room along with a few faithful. He turned up at the rulers' meeting wearing the armor he had covered with glory years earlier when he defended the city from the northern tribes.

"My loyal Ritti," said Haiff, "it seems both you and we are in the same boat. We gather there's been a riot in the city and even here inside the palace we are no longer safe. Many enemies are out to get us, so we must quickly act, crush them, and restore order, as we have done so often up to now."

"I am afraid it won't be all that easy this time, masters," the son of Karal spoke and everyone could see he was extremely worried. "The riot has spilled throughout the city and has come to nag us within this very palace where orders used to be obeyed unflinchingly. Myself I fear for my life. My spearmen no longer listen to my orders. In fact, they're after me right now, fully resolved to cut my throat. The palace is in their hands entirely, except for this wing that my men still have under control, though I have no idea how long they can hold."

"This can't be true. You can't be serious," the Great Ruler moaned. "Offer them money, Ritti. Hurry up and tell the spearmen they will get as much as they want.

Promise them anything. We can't afford to lose them now, with all that's going on outside. The rioters will certainly kill us on sight."

"Not necessarily, Great Haiff. My spies who were out there brought back astonishing reports. It seems that crazy prophet has given new laws to the city and there is one of them I think that might, for all its weirdness, save our lives."

"What are you talking about?" the High Priest scowled. "How dared this stranger change the laws of Nineveh? This man we could have killed and yet spared and released, how dared he incite the people to forget their old allegiance? Come on, commander, speak, you who instead of nipping the riot in the bud, preferred to hide and lock the door behind you like a frightened woman!"

"Hold it, High Priest!" the son of Karal cut him in. "I cannot be expected to put out by myself the fire you rulers have touched off hoping to fool the seven tribes. I'm afraid neither your money, nor your entire wealth will buy you back the spearmen that sided with the rioters. The one way out is still that law I was telling you about. The prophet had it written on a tablet and posted it out there for everyone to see and keep in mind."

"What law is this?" asked the Great Ruler impatiently. "Speak, Ritti!"

"Well, I am afraid this will upset you quite a bit, but the very first law they issued out there on the square said all of you, most noble rulers, including you, Great Haiff, and you, priest, were dead and done with, killed by the poison of your sins."

"We've heard about this nonsense. This is preposterous, of course," said the High Priest. "How can you count a living man among the dead? I, for one, have never felt so much alive in my whole life. Yes, we're alive and kicking and we will teach that moron, that would-be prophet, the difference between the living and the dead."

"We will too. How on earth could he even dream of such a law?" echoed the great Haiff.

"Just hear me out: you'll see how we can trap them with their own foolish laws," said the commander of the guard. "Look: their new law says the dead shall take no part in any business of the city, but there's another law that holds one shall respect the dead and never interfere with them or their inheritance. Anyone troubling the peace of the deceased shall be sentenced to a horrendous death himself. Now, do you get my point?"

"I'm not sure I see the meaning of all this," one of the rulers said in a puzzled voice. "Do you mean that by being considered dead we can walk out of here freely without anyone stopping us or hurting us or plundering our properties?"

"Exactly," exclaimed Ritti, son of Karal,. "We'll have to send a delegation to these usurpers and ask them to observe the laws they have just passed and leave the dead alone. I'm pretty sure their prophet will make a point of keeping up the new laws and press everyone else to do the same. If I am right, we'll walk across the square untroubled and although many of these rabble would be happy to strangle us with their bare hands, no one will even touch a hair on our heads."

"Well said, Ritti, my friend!" said the High Priest who knew a devious plot when he saw one. "I think we should send out the wise Nabir to be our envoy, as he appears to be on friendly terms with that wretched stranger. But where's Nabir? I haven't seen him since last night."

"The wise man sneaked out the back door before the rebel spearmen got hold of it. He must be far by now," explained Ritti.

"Here, here, there's yet another proof of his vile treachery!" cried the Great Ruler red with anger. "He must have joined the rioters. I'm sure he is the brain behind our misfortune."

"Then who are we going to send out there?" the rulers asked one another, as none of them felt bold enough to leave their hideout and face the rebel spearmen and the crowd outside.

"I'll go," said the son of Karal. "I am familiar with the secret passageways under the palace and with the hidden exits to the Lion's Pool and Tigris so I can reach close to their ragged prophet without being noticed. Wait for me quietly and make ready to leave the palace and go back to your homes as soon as you get my signal. I've been informed that many Ninevites are disappointed with the new rules. On our call, I'm sure they will rise up in arms and overturn the rebels."

The deposed rulers had not much of a choice, so they agreed to send out the commander of the guard as envoy and wait for the successful outcome of his mission. Ritti, son of Karal, picked one of his faithful servants and a couple of torches and vanished into the tortuous cellars of the palace. He knew his way all right and walked unhesitatingly along the twisted galleries up to a vaulted passage through the wall that opened on the square right near the Lions' Fountain.

A few men noticed them as they were pushing back the slab that masked the exit. They promptly recognized the spearmen's commander, who had tortured to death many of their relatives and friends, and fell on him with stones and daggers, but Ritti, son of Karal, was not a man to lose his head so easily.

"Hold your daggers, Ninevites! You, stubborn people, are you going to break your own new law? Go ahead, read it if you don't know it yet. It's on the tablets over there. It says that I, an unrepenting sinner, am a dead man and there's nothing you can do to me, or else you would disturb a dead man's peace, a capital offense, as you should know by now."

His assailers indeed stepped back, fearful to break the freshly instituted law and Ritti asked to see their leader, the new great ruler of the city. When the commander found him lying in the dust with two of his ex-spearmen watching him, he couldn't help bursting into laughter:

"Oh, righteous prophet, how come you're sleeping on the ground, you who were smart enough to take control of this great city? The palace right in front of you has dozens of richly furnished rooms. Aren't they good enough for you or are your feet suddenly turning cold and you don't dare to go and take what is not yours by right? With your glib talk you have unraveled in two days the laws we had observed for centuries. Do you by chance feel any remorse? You've wooed the people of Nineveh away from their duties and turned them into a stray fold with no shepherds. Aren't you afraid that lions will come out of the wilderness and rip this rowdy fold to pieces?"

He had been waiting for the guard commander. As the other was speaking, he stood up, shook the dust off his clothes and staring at his visitor he said:

"Alas, son of Karal! Your armor is as proud and your sword-wielding hand as nimble as your soul is dark with wickedness and crimes that cry for vengeance. You asked why I was lying in the dust rather than enter into the palace. Let me tell you I find this humble spot where the dogs of the city relieve themselves much cleaner than the great palace over there in which mischief and sin wriggle like restless worms. How dare you come like this in our midst, knowing that people hate you and many would be glad to take your life?"

"Most righteous ruler, I'm taking this chance as I trust the wise laws you have made and posted on this square. I'll be the first to test how fairly they apply in practice. In view of my great sins, the law regards me—and I regard myself—as dead. And since the law prohibits under tough penalty harming the dead in any way, here I am standing before you, requesting that the law be properly observed."

"I bet you're very proud of your cunning, son of Karal. If this is why you crept like a blind mole beneath the ground and surfaced like an evil spirit from behind those walls, go back and tell your fellows that the law I've made will fully be observed. Killed by your sins, let all of you come out of your dark lair and return to your homes. No one will hurt you on the way provided that you keep shouting all along that you are dead due to your sins. Those you have wronged will hear and refrain their vindictive impulse for fear of breaking the new law. You won't be harmed."

*   *   *

Around noontime, the big gates of the palace opened wide and a few guards still loyal to their chief, pointing their spears to the sky, lined up on both sides of the alley paved with marble slabs.

The High Priest Tamir walked out first. He glared at the curious crowd that packed the square and vented out his anger:

"Woe is you, stubborn sons of Nineveh! Your empty minds were easily beguiled into rebellion. The fathers of the city are scorned and chased today before your eyes. Do not rejoice, as you will have no one to turn to, no one to keep the old rules and provide for you. Your sons will starve and perish. The gods will visit their wrath on you and your offspring, and you will be accursed until the end of time."

Dazed by the hot noon sun, the crowd paid little attention to his words. Only a few in the front rows responded with some gibes and cursed him back. Most eyes instead were turned toward him, the strange researcher that had come out of the wilderness to be their prophet. He was standing alongside the seven lawmakers elected by the tribes and waited for the rulers' exit, but they were slow to show up. Following the eyes of the crowd, Tamir saw him and raising his gilded, ivory-handled staff in his direction thundered:

"You, wandering seer blown by an evil wind into our city, why are you doing this? Why do you trouble the people's minds and wreck their rules? Have you told them their temple will be closed tomorrow? There will be no one there to open it or take their offerings. You have incited them to drive me out, but who will bless their oil and spices?"

He gazed at the High Priest with understanding and, as the crowd was fidgeting and protesting around him, he raised his arm asking for silence and then said calmly:

"May you rest in peace, Tamir! As an erstwhile high priest of Nineveh, your death has made us sad. Too bad that your spirit passed away while your body still walks upon this earth."

"How dare you, good-for-nothing stranger, talk to me in this outrageous way?" the priest snarled back and went on in a rage, forgetting the petty stratagem on which their escape depended: "I am not dead at all. I am alive and I will see to it that you be sorry for these words."

"You're not alive, Tamir. You're just a dead man pestering the living. You may not know it, but the Scythians and Thracians think that the dead lurking around and harassing the living are ghosts and that there's no way to get rid of them except by sticking a dagger into their chest. Try to behave yourself as a dead person, or else the Ninevites may borrow this custom of the northern peoples. Once you have got a dagger between your ribs, there's nothing the new law can do for you. Go humbly home and no one will do you any harm. Go home and weep over your many sins, for that's the only way that you can still help save your city and clear your name that's written in the Book of Peoples. Walk in peace!"

He then turned to the crowd that was, for once, completely quiet, as everyone was anxious not to miss a thing, and said:

"Someone lend him a donkey. He's got quite a long way to go."

But Tamir did not wait for the donkey. Turning his back on the prophet, he nervously elbowed his way through the crowd followed by a few servants that had come to meet him at the gate.

The former Great Ruler Haiff and Bubu the wheat merchant got out last. Like everybody else, they had listened to the exchange between the prophet and Haiff, so they walked out furiously but quietly heading straight home.

The flighty crowd exulted over the victory of their uprising. Then, after some vacillation, pushing one another, they started running to the gate and trampling on some spearmen that tried to stop them, poured into the palace yard and on into the lavish rooms. Bedazzled, they set off breaking the precious vases, ripping the gilt-thread woven tissues off the walls, maiming the statues and the bas-reliefs they couldn't overturn. Many of the rioters, however, perceived it as a splendid opportunity to make a fortune and bundled up as many valuable things as they could carry or stashed them here and there hoping to come back and collect them later on. Ritti, son of Karal, and his few loyal spearmen tried unsuccessfully to put up some resistance. Overwhelmed with blows, they finally retreated to the back rooms and vanished through the underground galleries that opened up into the bushes on the riverbanks.

He and the seven lawmakers elected by the tribes were just as powerless to stem the rush. Outtalking them, the thugs of Nineveh were now leading the pack and their calls to loot and mayhem were music to the willing crowd. Eventually, he rallied a few people and, at dusk, together with the guards that had not run away, they managed to lock and bolt the palace gates from the outside. Once again, the supporters of the new law saw themselves on the fountain square while a new enemy was locked inside the palace.

* * *

In the rulers' palace the plunderers were raising Cain. Fighting for booty, they soon got down to killing one another. A well-known robber surrounded by his thugs was crying out loud this was all right. This was the law, he said: let anyone grab what they can; the strong get more, the weak get less if anything at all. The farsighted, however, did not care about the loot, but wanted to seize power and clustering in shady corners of the palace debated who should have which office.

Gripping a torch in his healthy hand and mounting on the plinth of a statue the crowd had just knocked down, Salak, an alert one-armed crook, that tithed every beggar in the city, shouted he was the best choice for a treasurer.

But then one man turned up dashing everyone else's plans. Freed by his goons, Bendal, son of Saiq, the terror of the land, who'd robbed about every merchant in the city, emerged on his men's shoulders from the palace jail. Amid hurrahs they begged him to become the leader of the mob and organize them to grab power in Nineveh. Though weakened by his time in prison, the bandit was quick to seize the opportunity. Snatching a large copper basin the palace servants used for washing their feet, but which his men had filled with wine, he quaffed greedily, then soaked his face and woolly beard into the drink and shook off like a wet dog, splashing everyone around and roaring with laughter.

"Brothers," he thundered and suddenly the looting hordes were still. "Brothers! Listen to me and I'll make you all rich and carefree. Since the rulers have fled and we are reveling inside this palace at which many of you were even too afraid to look, I reckon it is we the real rulers of Nineveh and can do what we please as of right now. So I say we should bunch up into gangs and storm into the merchants' houses claiming tithe. And whoever resists let him be tortured until he spills out where his money's hidden and when we clean him out, let him be killed along with his entire household and his house set on fire as a lesson for others, so that they don't balk when our men turn up claiming the tax."

"Yes, yes, let's do so!" some of the thugs yelled tottering on their feet, as everyone had swilled their fill of the strong wine they had discovered in the palace cellars.

"Let's do so," Salak echoed from his plinth. "But put this into your minds that you can't find a better treasurer than me."

"Take him down from there and cut his head off," Bendal exclaimed as he caught sight of the crook. "This bastard has wronged and spoiled every cripple in town."

"He did, he did!" the audience noisily confirmed and some of them rushed to the plinth, but the one-armed man was quicker: jumping down from his platform, he vanished into the darkness of the yard, among the bushes.

The city's small-time thieves were busy currying favor with Bendal, recalling his great feats and even bringing him the Great Ruler's jewel-studded seat from where they'd cached it. They did have quite some trouble carrying the throne among the kleptomaniac crowd that flocked around the famous bandit and had to club on their way dozens of hands that tried to pry out the glittering stones with their bare nails or the points of their knives.

Bendal thanked them and sat haughtily in the Great Ruler's seat, asking that they fetch him a gold cup filled with the best of wines they could find in the cellar. His order once swiftly carried out, he sipped from the heavy goblet, smacked his lips, and said:

"Now, brothers, what about picking ourselves a king?"

"You're the best. We need no other king than you," cried one of his jail mates that had been doing time for many crimes and would have still been in chains but for that fortunate uprising.

"You're absolutely right, Haler. Come sit by me. I am appointing you my chief adviser," said the freshly anointed king and pulled a long swill on his goblet letting the precious wine swirl down his beard and chest.

A beggar with small foxy eyes approached him cautiously and stopping within reverent distance gave a low bow.

"What is it, Sinareb"

"Pardon me, noble king, but your throne will not be safe as long as that alien prophet is still out there on the square. We beggars find his teachings quite upsetting. Imagine that! He's planning to have us rounded up and put to do chores. For the public good, as he said in his nutty law. How can a beggar work?"

Bendal burst into laughter, then turned to the beggar seriously and said:

"Happy are you, Sinareb, for you're the first one to address me as your king! I'll make you a rich man. You won't have to worry about anything from now on. You will no longer rummage in the trash dumps with the rats. Now tell me what you know about that prophet. I've heard about him a few things and even caught a glimpse of him while he was down there in jail."

"Great king, he's been here for no longer than two days and look what's happened. Not that we're sorry for the former rulers or anything, but even the old law has crumbled. Now he has had the palace gates locked from the outside and I fear we might have some trouble getting out, as many Ninevites are still on his side."

"We'll take care of him at dawn tomorrow," Bendal said confidently. "We're going to stone him to death and crush every tablet on which he's had his silly laws inscribed."

"Yeah, let's do so! Let's do so!" cried several voices heavily imbibed while a few torches rose toward the black sky.

A hooded man stepped forth from the crowd and stopped before the jewel-studded seat. Lifting his hood, he asked:

"Is that you the leader of this unruly mob?"

"By all means, I'm he," Bendal replied in a swaggering voice. "I am the king of Nineveh. What do you want?"

"I am the trusted servant of High Priest Tamir. My master wants to talk with you. He said he could teach you quite a few things that would be useful to you if you wanted to be the king of Nineveh."

Bendal gazed at him bleary-eyed from the strong wine. After a short silence, he asked cagily:

"Where is this master of yours?"

"He's waiting for you in a safe place. I'll take you there to meet him."

"No way. You tell him I'm the king now and I'm going nowhere. If he wants to talk to me, let him appear before my throne and I will hear him."

"Out of the question. My master fears for his life."

"Let him fear then. What do I care about his life? Did he care about mine while I lay in prison? Go tell him I'll be here at the palace if he desires to see me."

"I'll tell him so, sir," the servant said and bowed. Then shrouding back his face he melted into the crowd.

Behind his back, Bendal bragged with a tickled grin: He was a great king, wasn't he, if the High Priest wanted to talk with him? He had no way to know that the sly Tamir had already sent messages to Babylon and the Medes, calling on them to march their armies on the city.

Late at night when the buzz of the city had died away, only a handful of people were still listening to the prophet's teachings around a feeble fire near the Lions' Pool. His heart was grieving for everything that had happened and even more so for what he knew was still to come. His efforts to make the Ninevites amend had sadly failed. He had almost entirely lost hope to save the city or the tablets. Wearily, he lay down by the moribund fire and went asleep.

*   *   *

As he woke up on a heap of dusty papers in the chairman's office, he couldn't make out whether he had fainted or just dozed off. He should have been mighty glad that he was in the chilly tower rather than back in Nineveh where Bendal's thugs were out to kill him. It had been just a dream, of course, but he didn't like the way it ended. Actually, he ached to return to the ancient city and save the tablets, as the voice had ordered him out there in the wilderness.

Outside the wind was blowing harder and harder in the darkness, making the tower tremble like a twig. He could hear the frozen gusts whistling and shrieking through the metal rings of the atom. Still perched, as though forgotten, on the roof, it had little to do with what was going on below. In fact, nothing was going on below. They were keeping it up there as a front to mislead people into thinking something was still happening in Tower B. As if it knew all this, the metal ghost seemed to be wailing in distress under the blizzard.

Somewhere inside a door kept banging in the wind. He tried to remember if he'd closed the door to the terrace, but wasn't sure of it any more and thought he'd better go up and check. Some light would have been useful and he found his candle stub all right, but the matches were gone, probably lost. He was cold and his feet had grown numb. He understood there was no point trying to leave the tower, but lying motionless in the cold was not a good idea either. He had to find himself some warmer place and wait until the morning. He would more easily get out of this maze in the daylight. Meanwhile the library he thought might be a better shelter. The walls were lined with bookshelves and books are known to make a quite good insulator. Books do not give up to frost so easily: they fight; occasionally they even win.

He groped out of the chairman's office, found the banister, and started tottering downstairs. Every step down was like sinking into nothingness. The wind moaned so piercingly that he could barely hear the cat mewing behind him as if he tried to caution him: "Watch your steps, my friend, lest you fall down again!" By the heap of rubble on which he stumbled on the landing, he knew he'd reached the library floor. He felt the walls around and found the doorjamb. He had been wrong about the library. It was even colder than the chairman's office: many windows were broken or didn't close and the wind was furiously sweeping loads of snow inside. He tried to shut the door but it was stuck and he was too weak to move it. The descent had sucked up what little force he had left. He felt dizzy again and sat down on a pile of books to rest a bit.

No sooner had he caught his breath than the general manager called him to account. He was sort of inspecting the library apparently. He shouldn't have taken photos of the icicles hanging from the bookshelves, yelled the big boss. The rules of the institute made it crystal-clear: the employees shall in no circumstances photograph the library icicles without the management's express approval.

He stammered he had just been trying to give a hand with defrosting those books, but the general manager was pissed and would not even listen to him. He said he'd wasted too much time on him already and was going to turn him over to the intelligence guys and prosecutors. The general manager was just as cold as he was. He was wearing a sort of knitted cap pulled down over his ears and kept breathing into his hands to warm them while he repeated on and on, "You must give me the film. Do you hear me? Give me the original film. Give it to me right now!"

He gave him the full camera just to get him off his back. The general manager seemed quite content. He stashed the camera into a safe cabinet. There was no point anyone else should see that photo of the library in icicles, he said: he already had too many enemies watching his every step like polecats.

Suddenly the Father Researcher turned up saying he was looking for a book, but as he turned to find it for him, he saw the library was running amok again: some of the books were turning into boards and sawdust, while others glittered on the shelves as though they were ablaze. He wondered how a thing like that could happen. Was there a scientific explanation? The father put an end to his bewilderment:

"Those books the science of which was desacralized by human mind are reverting to wood, which their paper had been made of, and their contents will be forever lost. Those in which science and the sacred were not cut off from each other will shine and last over the centuries and enlighten human minds."

As he was wondering what he was supposed to do, the father asked him point-blank:

"Have you not been ordered to rescue from the invaders' hands the tablets enshrining the primeval wisdom of the peoples?"

"I have, but—" he hesitated, then confessed ashamedly: "I don't know how to get back to Nineveh. I can no longer find the path and that blizzard that has been raging outside frightens me."

"Find the path and return. The science written on those tablets is an example to every researcher of the new century, for it was not desacralized by human mind. Everything was still sacred in Nineveh when those tablets were made."

"I am afraid I will be killed if I go back," he said in a feeble voice. "Many enemies are plotting to take my life. I am surrounded from all sides."

"You have lost hope and your strength has gone with it," the father scolded him. "Go back and fight to the end, or else you'll never be anything but a poor researcher lost between centuries; you'll never join the number of those that are investigating the new century. Strive and come join the scientists that are enlightened by the truth!"

As the father walked out of the library, he was terribly cold again and huddled between two piles of books trying to take some rest. He was growing increasingly more tired every minute. What little strength he had left now seemed to ooze out of his body and he felt he could no longer move his arms. Finally, he didn't even care about the cold anymore. He felt light as a feather and his thoughts were flying to Nineveh where he was anxious to return and carry out the order given him in the wilderness.

7

A GHASTLY WIND WAS UP AND black clouds had covered the sky plunging the city into darkness. The frightened Ninevites were running along the streets, worried about their families and fortunes. All by himself near the Lions' Pool, he was staring sadly at the tablets on which the new laws had been written. They lay scattered and broken all over the square. The people had trampled on them in their stampede.

He then could see how Bendal, king of the thieves, had woken from his drunken stupor. His mates brandishing spears and daggers were asking for his permission to go and waste the alien prophet. But Bendal disagreed and promised a bagful of gold to whoever captured the prophet alive, as he was set on having him tortured to death according to Assyrian customs.

He got scared and suddenly lost the power he had been given just as suddenly on his arrival in the city. He could no longer see through walls or hear what was being said far from his ears' reach. Neither was he allowed any longer to slip out of his body and roam where his mind carried him.

"Woe is me, sinner that I am!" he moaned. "My spirit has bent like a reed in the wind and my faith went out like a lamp that has run out of oil. Now I will be easily caught and slain, for I can no longer see which way my enemies are coming or learn about their crafty plots."

As he was crying over his fate, a pat on his shoulder made him start. He turned and saw a man wrapped up in goatskins, bearing a staff of fire in his hand. His hair was like a yarn of hemp and eyes like emeralds stared piercingly from his face so white as if made of sea foam.

"Are you the prophet recently arrived in Nineveh to urge the people to repentance?" asked the man.

"Alas, I am no kind of prophet," he replied beating upon his chest. "I can only tell what I see but now my power is lost because my spirit wavered and I am like a helpless child. I'm back to what I used to be—a powerless researcher at the turn of the century."

The man raised one arm toward the sky rent by lightning and said:

"Open your eyes and look! The city walls collapse washed out by the floods. The armies of the enemy pour in. Chariots storm through the streets. The soldiers have red shields and their spears are like broaches brandishing infants ripped off their mothers' arms. The women tear their hair out with grief while the men are taken into bondage. The shining palaces are dust and ashes and the spoils are rich: gold and silver are sacked and plundered. Blood and ashes are everywhere. The grandeur of Nineveh has fallen apart forever and her enemies rejoice. This is the true prophecy; this is what is written and this is what will come to pass."

"What about me? What am I to do?" he asked looking around him in confusion.

"Hurry up and leave while you still can. The city gates are giving way and the bloodbath is about to start."

"I tremble to hear you, great prophet, but I can't leave until I carry out my order. The tablets on which the very earliest wisdom of the world is written—they need to be saved."

"Forget about your big, proud plans," the goatskin-clad man urged him. "The wisdom of this world is but a drop within the boundless ocean of true knowledge. Tarry no more! Go now while you still can and have the force to leave. I can already see the Medes up north and the armies of Babylon as they pull together to fall upon the city and put Nineveh to the sword." Upon these words, the man vanished from sight, while his glowing staff rose up into the air setting the sky ablaze.

He was frightened. The enemies were on their way and there was no other escape for him than to leave at once. Instead of that, he remembered the wise Nabir had offered him the hospitality of his home in case he ever needed a shelter. He hoped the stargazer was all right and his offer still stood. As he was heading for the wise man's house, rivers of rain started pouring down from the sky and big lumps of ice fell rattling on the pavement slabs. He sought cover behind a wall and stood there waiting quite a while until the furor of the storm abated.

When he arrived at the stargazer's house, the night had fallen. He pounded on the tall gate and shouted as loud as he could for a long time. At last, toting a sword, a sullen slave appeared and inspected him through a peephole.

"Go away, stranger! The master's ordered we let no one in."

"Go tell your master the researcher that has to save the city library is here to see him. Deliver this message quickly and he will receive me."

He waited anxiously in the rain. Thunders clattered and flashes of lightning ripped the gloomy sky while water cascaded down the roofs and across streets and yards washing everything away.

"Take care, stranger!" the slave cautioned him as he was opening the gate. "The master will see you all right, but his heart is heavy, so don't add any more burdens to his grief."

He found the wise Nabir pacing his summer bedroom like a caged lion. Fear was written all over his pale face.

"My righteous friend, am I glad to see you! I was afraid those rogues that took the palace might have killed you."

"The Lord my God has saved my life from yet another peril. But my heart doubted and was overcome with fear and therefore I am punished now. My powers are lost: my eyes can't see except what is before them; my ears no longer hear what my enemies are plotting."

"Everything happens as ordained," the wise man said with a sigh. "We humans are only given omens and forebodings and only if we're worthy of them."

"You spoke the truth, wise man! The last time I received a sign I was alone and hopeless in the storm. A man holding a staff of fire talked to me. He told me the oracle concerning Nineveh. I won't sadden your heart with any details, but the end will be frightening."

"I know, my righteous friend," Nabir said mournfully. "I'm well aware of prophet Nahum's vision. He saw and portrayed in full gory detail the ruin of our city. I think it must have been Nahum himself that talked to you. His prophecy, alas, seems to be coming true to the letter. The rain will soon make the river overflow and rush against the city walls bringing them down, right as the prophet said. Two years ago, Cyaxares, king of the Medes, conquered our city of Ashur. Nabopolassar, the chief commander of our troops, sold us out, conspiring with the Medes and Babylonians to attack us. They say it is his son, Nebuchadnezzar, who was brought up amongst us and knows Nineveh inside out, including its fortifications and weak points, it's he they say that will command the army of Babylon. Didn't the prophet tell you warriors clad in scarlet would defeat us? It is the color of Babylon's foot soldiers. The Rulers' Palace has fallen to robbers and the defenders of the city are all scattered. Woe is us, for our sins are visited upon us! Woe is Nineveh!"

"Wise Nabir, wails and regrets are no good in this terrible hour. They say that as the spirit weakens and gives way to fear, the body will be weakened too and enemies will shortly have the best of it. Lift up your heart then and shake off this fear that has got hold of you. Tell me, what is this all about? Why are your servants gathering all your treasures and heaping everything outside this room? What is it that your slaves are hauling in those big copper pails and spreading on your things? Is it that black fat of the earth that quickly goes ablaze? Are you going to set on fire all your lifetime's wealth?"

"My righteous friend, everybody knows we Assyrians, particularly we Ninevites, have treated ruthlessly the residents of every city we have conquered. Our soldiers callously killed women and children, flayed people and stretched their skins on the walls, stabbed darts into their eyes and chests. As for the leaders of those cities, our soldiers chopped off their hands and feet and let them agonize and rot in cages. I won't allow that I or any member of my household goes through this. So I decided we'll be better off burning everything on the pyre, ourselves included, before the enemies lay hands on us and torture us for their entertainment."

"I can understand your fear, wise man, but wouldn't it be worthier of you to perish fighting to defend your city rather than torch yourself to an inglorious death? All my efforts to save the city have been unsuccessful, but I still have to carry out the order given me in the wilderness. That's why I'm here. You swore by the luminaries of the sky that you would help me salvage those treasures Nineveh possessed that were more valuable than all her gold and greatness. Now, here I am, falling on my knees before you and begging you to take me where they are. The ancient tablets on which humanity's very primeval truths are written must be saved. Otherwise they will perish with the city and truth itself will be forever lost."

Nabir engrossed in thoughts was silent for a while. It seemed the storm that raged outside was also playing havoc with his mind.

"In truth," the wise man said at last. "I did swear to take you where those tablets were and help you rescue them. I am among the few who know the way. What you are looking for is right inside the palace that's in the robbers' power at present. The library of the great king Ashurbanipal, in which those ancient tablets have been kept, is in that lair of thieves, but they can't harm it, as all the entrances were walled off shortly before the king died. Besides, it's common knowledge the king himself had the place stripped of any gold and silver ornaments, to make sure that whoever in the future tore down the wall did so not for the sake of worldly treasures but rather in a quest for truth and wisdom."

"The great king was a wise and prudent man indeed. The wall that blocks the entrance to the library is safe as far as robbers are concerned, for they're not after wisdom, but the Babylonians might want to tear it down in order to retrieve their own possessions."

"That's true," Nabir confirmed. "Many of the tablets are war spoils from way back when our king destroyed proud Babylon. I wonder what can be done right now. I'm thinking of a way to—"

"Think, wise man, think! There must be a way and you know it. Once the Babylonians pour in, they'll dash everything to pieces. Palaces, if they are demolished, others even more magnificent will be built instead, but if the clay tablets are destroyed, those writings will be lost for all eternity; ignorance will take the place of knowledge; oblivion will replace remembrance; falsehood will substitute for truth, and folly will succeed to wisdom. This is the real threat looming over this city. Towers and palaces may be razed so that not one stone is left on another and the sand of the desert may bury them forever, but if the tablets last, they will be testimony of your life and Nineveh will live in people's minds long after it has been destroyed."

"My dear friend, your plea has moved me. Your words have struck the chord of truth. I used to spend a lot of time in the king's library. The king himself had noticed my eagerness to learn, so shortly before his death he told me about a secret tunnel from the library leading outside the palace walls. I took an oath to keep this secret but I will break it tonight so I can keep my other oath to you. I see that you, albeit a stranger, are keen on saving what is ours and of which we should take care ourselves. This has decided me. Let's to the library before it is too late."

The wise Nabir girded on his sword and ordered three of his servants to take up arms and follow him. Upon his orders, they prepared a chariot and torches, and added two cedar beams and a ball of strong rope. Before leaving, Nabir sent for Batusasareb, head of his servants, and told him in front of everyone:

"My faithful servant, I know your loyalty and how you've always taken good care of my property while I was away. I have heard no reports of you wronging anyone or punishing an innocent. Tonight I'm leaving on an errand more dangerous than any I have faced so far. I might never be back. If I do not return by noon tomorrow or send you notice by that time, you'll count me dead. In that case, you will bolt the doors so that no one comes in or goes out any longer, take the ivory-hilted dagger I gave you as a present, and do what I would have done myself. Then you'll set fire. No property of mine—whether a child, a concubine, a wife, a cow, a weapon, or a goblet—shall fall into the hands of Babylon. Once you have carried out this one last order, you will be free to do anything you like."

"My body will burn along with those of all the others," the head servant assured him, tears welling in his eyes. He then kneeled and kissed his master's sandals, while Nabir put his hands over his head and blessed him.

Finally, they got into the chariot that had been packed with everything they needed and set off along the silent streets. No one dared to go out where the rain kept pouring mercilessly. The chariot rolled around the palace walls and along the canal that flows from the Khusur into the Tigris. The wise Nabir asked it be stopped before a rock in a small grove. On their master's orders, the servants tied the rock to the chariot and using the cedar beams as pries, made it slide over in the mud baring the secret entrance.

"Kill the horses and throw them into the river," Nabir ordered. "Take my precious chariot apart and dump the pieces into the water. I don't want my enemies to find it and brag that they have slain me and seized away my things."

Under the heavy rain, the servants silently did as they were told. When they were done, they lit the torches and they climbed down all five into a narrow tunnel that ran beneath the riverbed and palace wall. Nabir was obviously familiar with the place, for he had his marks on the walls and any time they crossed another tunnel, he knew which way to go. At last, they came up to a slab door flanked by bull's heads, one on each side. As the wise man slowly turned the right-hand one around, the heavy slab slid smoothly aside and a small vaulted room opened before them. There was nothing in it except a winding stair they climbed up to a door plated with copper scales.

"Here is the library of the great King Ashurbanipal. No one has troubled the peace of this place since his death," said the wise man pulling out a key from his belt. He had to push until the door creaked slowly open and they walked into an immense hall the vaults of which rested on marble columns. The servants' torches first lit two large winged, human-headed lions that framed the door. They entered then into a maze of shelves made of thick gilded boards on which masses of clay tablets were carefully arranged. Gripping a servant's torch, Nabir climbed up a flight of steps, walked around, and stopped by a huge stone platform on which thousands of tablets were displayed. Guarding the platform were four statues of eagle-headed warriors.

"My dear, truth-loving researcher, here is what you are looking for and answers to your every question. The science and wisdom of the ancient peoples lies before your eyes."

"Oh wise man, I don't know if you can understand my happiness: my one wish has come true. I wonder how we can move these tablets to a secret place where they can live on safely for the great benefit of coming generations. I am afraid Bendal's lowlifes who must be ransacking the palace will come upon the wall that hides this place and tear it down. I think we'd better move everything away to a safe place. Not just these tablets, all of them. I'm sure they will be very valuable over the years."

"It can't be done," Nabir replied. "We would need at least two thousand wagons to carry everything that's in here. Besides, where would we carry them? And how would such a convoy slip away unnoticed by the Babylonians? But there's a cache right beneath our feet, where we could hide some of the tablets. At least the ancient ones that lie upon that platform would be saved. It's covered by a huge slab that can be moved away unless it's locked. It only locks from the inside. It means one of us will have to go down there and lock himself up with the tablets. And die there, I suppose."

"I'll be the one," he said without the slightest hesitation. "It's I that have been ordered to take care of these writings and I intend to do so through and through. I'll keep a torch, so I will have the privilege of poring over them untroubled to the last."

The wise Nabir walked to the winged, human-headed lions and turned their necks around, first the right-hand one and then the other. The slab that masked the entrance to the cache was actually a huge stone block showing a bas-relief of battle scenes. Nabir ordered his servants to push hard. Finally, it budged uncovering a narrow passage through which a man could barely slip inside. Gripping a torch, the wise Assyrian entered first and they filed in behind him climbing down two flights of stairs.

"This is where the great King Ashurbanipal planned to hide his treasures in case of extreme danger. As you can see, there are no treasures: it's empty like a barren tomb. I think this is the best place where we can put the tablets. No one—neither the Babylonians nor Bendal's thieves— will come to look for them in here."

The statue of a bull rose in one corner of the room. Nabir pointed at it and said:

"Take care, my righteous friend! Our lives hang on that yonder bull's horns. Those horns can turn everything above us into ruins."

"What do you mean, wise man?"

"Listen carefully, for you must know. In the end, you'll have to pull hard on these horns until they turn around. As they do so, the slab that blocks the entrance will slide back and then the columns that sustain the ceiling of the library will budge and the whole place will crumble. Everything you saw up there will turn into a mound of debris."

He shuddered for a moment, but then he told himself nothing would happen that had not been ordained beforehand.

"Let's get down to work, will you!" he urged them. "Let's carry the most valuable tablets down here."

They put the torches into holders along the steps and then Nabir and his three men went upstairs and started carrying the tablets to the passage in the wall wherefrom he took them down and stacked them in the cache.

They worked all night carrying some twenty-five thousand tablets until the platform guarded by eagle-headed warriors was empty. At dawn their palms bled and their arms hung wearily. They were all in the library upstairs and had stopped for a minute to catch their breaths when muted whomps were heard on the other side of the wall that Ashurbanipal had built to isolate the library from the palace. The wise man was so weary that he didn't trust his senses anymore.

"Do you hear what I hear or am I just imagining things?" he asked.

"You're not mistaken, master," one of the servants answered. "They're tearing down the wall to get here."

"It must be the Babylonians," Nabir said gloomily. "Who else would care about the library? I'm only astonished that they should have conquered the city so easily. I didn't expect they would be here so soon."

"Woe is us, master!" one of the servants moaned. "If the Medes and Babylonians are already in the palace, then Nineveh must be awash with blood and all our people dead or being killed right now."

"I am afraid it must be so, my faithful servant. It has to be the enemy, for no one among the Ninevites would dig his way into the library. Everybody knows the king stored nothing here but writings. Bendal and his mates must be aware of it like anybody else. They wouldn't knock down walls to look for treasures where they know there is none."

Meanwhile the bangs were coming closer and Nabir felt that farewell time had come. He turned to him and said:

"It's time to part, my righteous friend. We've done together a good job. But now I think you'd better slip downstairs and hearken carefully and when there's no more rattling of swords up here, it will be time to close. My men and I will wait here for the enemy and fight them to the last. We are Assyrians and owe it to our gods and law. You are a stranger and have other duties to your own God and law. Adieu!"

The wise man hugged him, clapped his shoulders, then turned to his servants and urged them to get ready:

"Gird up your loins and draw your swords! Whoever falters let his name be cursed forever."

As he was saying so, he gripped a torch and holding out his naked sword walked to the wall where bricks were coming out already. With every blow from the outside the breach was gapping wider.

"Who are you that dare disturb the peace of the great king's library?" Nabir asked in a threatening voice, ready to strike.

On the other side the blows stopped suddenly, as the demolishers were probably stunned to hear a voice in a place they had good reason to suppose was empty.

"Speak up! Who are you, miserable slaves?" Nabir asked once again. "How dare you tear down the king's palace?"

A dusty bearded robber's face poked out the hole.

"The king has ordered us to open up this hallway," he said.

"What king?" Nabir asked in astonishment. "The city of Nineveh has yet to elect a king. The rulers' council has not yet decided who should succeed the great Ashurbanipal, blessed be his memory."

Jeers and laughter came from beyond the wall.

"We have already elected our king," several voices cried. "Bendal, son of Saiq, is our king and a mighty great king he is, too."

Nabir was downhearted.

"Alas, poor Nineveh! The foreign enemy has not yet come within sight of your walls and you already stand defeated by your own blood." He was still puzzled, though. "Why did your king send you to break into the library? Don't you all know there's no gold, or silver in this room? All you will find is clay tablets that you can't read or understand."

"It is the tablets we are sent for," said the bearded fellow who was halfway into the library by now. "These tablets of baked clay are very useful to us now. The river has overflowed and washed away part of the palace wall. Bendal said we should mend it with the tablets. He is afraid the Babylonians might burst into the palace through the breach."

"Unlawful and unlearned ruffians, how can you even think of using as vile bricks these tablets on which the scribes have patiently incised sage teachings over centuries?"

"We know what we are doing. We're nowhere near as dumb as you consider us to be, wise guy," exclaimed one of the robbers who, poking his head out the hole, seemed to have recognized Nabir. "The tablets are well baked. Water won't soften them as it did to the unbaked bricks that lay at the foundation of the wall."

"Come on, brothers. Save your breaths," urged an unseen character, their boss apparently, from behind. "The Babylonians may be here any minute now. Besides, the king has given us an order that we must carry out."

Hammers and axes resumed their banging right away and the hole broadened rapidly. Soon enough the robbers broke into the library and crossed swords with Nabir and his servants that were trying to repel them.

He had remained transfixed behind a column watching the fight while more and more robbers were pouring in surrounding the valiant defenders of the library. The servants were quickly overwhelmed and fell under the blows, but Nabir, a skilful blade, still stood his ground, drawing the enemies among the columns which he used as cover, and thinning their numbers. Finally, as he found himself trapped, back to the wall, he shouted out:

"Now, go ahead, my friend! Take the bull by the horns!"

These were the wise man's last words before the robbers had the best of him and, as they echoed loudly under the vaults, he knew the time had come. Swiftly, he sneaked among the tablet shelves and vanished through the narrow door into the cache. The assailants, who realized one of Nabir's men was still hiding somewhere, began to search for him. Down there, he found himself before the bull. A torch the servants had left behind was still burning and he could see the bronze horns gleam under its shimmer. Unhesitatingly, he grasped them both and mustering up his strength twisted them forcefully. Presently, he heard the stone block creaking shut. Moments later, there was a violent tremor followed by a deafening rumble, as though the sky was crashing on the palace. He knew up there everything was crumbling—the columns and the big stone vault. He was not afraid anymore. He was glad he had done his duty, carried out the mission he had been assigned back in the wilderness. He was actually happy for having saved so many tablets. The entire huge library had collapsed over the cache. There was no way out. He was trapped in there as though in a tomb. So in the short time he had left he thought he could as well take a look at those writings and see what he had saved.

He picked a few tablets at random, held them close to the torch, and slowly began to decipher their inscriptions. One of them was nothing but a sequence of names and he assumed it was a list of the library stock. Gilgamesh was there and so was Hammurabi's code of laws. He started searching for the tablets that were of highest interest to him: those that contained the early scientific knowledge He would have liked to read them all, but had no time to do so, as a powerful bang woke him up.

He was still huddling on a pile of books in the Tower B library. He could hear hammer blows and the rasping sound of metal dragged on the stairs coming from one of the upper floors. A faint light sifted in from outside. He couldn't realize whether it was twilight or dawn; he had lost count of time. He felt as though he'd been there for ages lying on heaps of books among the upset shelves. At some point, the wind must have blown strongly through the open window, for he was covered up with snow. He would have liked to rise and shake it off, but had no strength to do so. His arms and legs were failing him. The eyes alone could still move in their sockets and he could still hear what was going on around him. He could see Isaac, for example. Perched on a shelf, with bristling tail, the tomcat lay in wait ready to snap at two doves that were cooing unwittingly on a pile of journals. He would have liked to scold the cat, tell him this was bad conduct, but he could speak no more.

Some gypsies with sledgehammers entered into the room. He recognized them: he had seen them before as they were up to stealing manhole covers. They were plundering the tower now, stealing the rusty radiators that had been out of use for years. Spitting in their hands, they set off tearing the heavy cast iron heaters from the walls. Their hammers banging on the coils made a hell of a noise. One of them started flinging his club at the doves that were fluttering madly through the room trying to make it to the window. Upset that his prey had flown, Isaac was mewing.

"Hey, look, a black cat. That's bad luck."

"Forget about the cat, man. Look what I've got here. A stiff. Oh, I'll be fucked, man, he ain't dead. He just zonked out. Come, baby, let your daddy see what you got on you!"

Numb as he was, there was no way he could resist, as the mustached gypsy rolled him around like a potato sack and searched him thoroughly. There was nothing to find.

"Fuck, fuck, fuck! Nothing, man, he's got nothing. No ring, no golden teeth, no poke, no cell phone. Don't even have a fucking watch. Every jerk has a watch, man. I know who he is, this shit. He's gotta be one of those dicks that used to mess around here with their fucking atomic stuff."

Eventually, the gypsy let him be, but he had turned him face to the floor and now he could no longer see what they were doing. He heard them drag the radiators out and roll them banging down the steps. Then some of them came back with sacks that they began to load with something. He couldn't see what it was, but found out soon enough. Said one: "Don't take the little ones, you dope. Take them that has big sheets that's good for cornets." And then another one replied: "The little ones' good too. You kindle fire in the stove with 'em."

Where he was lying there were many big broad-paged books that would have made great cornets for their sunflower seeds. Indeed they noticed them and rolled him over to pick the ones under his body. He lay face up again so he could see them bending over him but could feel nothing when they took off his boots and clothes. They went away then, hauling the book sacks on their shoulders and, as they were climbing down the steps, he could still hear them wrangling over which of them would have his boots.

The room was very quiet now. He was no longer on the floor but seemed to be somehow suspended from, or perhaps floating near, the ceiling. Astonished and with a sense of helplessness, he looked down at the blue, naked body sprawled out on the books. Isaac the cat stood watching by its head, mewing eerily, as if he wanted to bring charge against the gypsies that had plundered the library and filched the man's clothes. From up there, he himself thought that he should report the robbery, but there was no one to report to. They were all gone. The tower was deserted except for Isaac and an owl screeching ominously on a windowsill. It was winter outside. To him it was most certainly the last.

He didn't mind. It had been a long harsh winter anyway, so he was glad to see Nabir coming to pick him in a new shining chariot. The wise man wore white clothes with gold embroidery and chamois sandals. He looked quite cheerful as though he cared no longer that Nineveh was gone, that its proud towers had turned to dust, that its big gates named after the Assyrian gods were lost forever, buried in the desert sand.

"We did a good job back there," the wise man told him. "The tablets that we saved have been unearthed by archeologists and are displayed with honors in the British Museum. They are the testimony of the grandeur of Nineveh and a good number of researchers rake their brains to understand their writings."

He himself was still barefoot and naked, as he'd been left after the gypsies mugged him. He didn't care about the clay tablets anymore. He now felt sorry for the library books in Tower B that would end up as cornets and he was angry there was nothing he could do to stop this.

His anger quickly vanished, as they arrived on a green meadow strewn with flowers where sundry kinds of birds were chirping joyfully. There was a grassy common on the meadow and a canal running across it that tapped on seven artesian wells along its way. The water jets with sunbow crowns on top of them were glistening in the sun. A herd of fat cows with full udders were grazing on the common. He soon discovered the two lads that guarded them. They were less skinny than they used to be. They fared much better now and did not lunch on cucumbers and cold polenta any longer. Their bags were full of chocolates, cookies, wafers, and all sorts of sweets their parents had been giving in remembrance. They crunched no more sunflower seeds either. Apparently one of them had fallen sick with appendicitis because of them. His parents didn't know what was wrong with him and there was no physician in their village, so when they took him to hospital in town it was too late. The other boy kept gazing at some dry elms along the border of the wood. The winter had been hard there too, he said. If only the forest guard had let his father fell those elms and take them home to burn; if only they had not put his dad under criminal inquiry for those dry elms, his folks and he could have stayed warm part of the winter and maybe he would never have had that trouble with his lungs.

How come he knew those boys, asked the wise Nabir. They were his playmates as a kid, he said and it was only then he realized both the Assyrian and he were kids again and thinking of some game to play. Their herdsmen friends insisted they play ball. They meant *clinch'ya*, the kind of game they played back home. They said it was all right, as *clinch'ya* is best played in twos—two batters and two runners.

He left the game early. He was eager to go back to his mother and father and grandparents he hadn't seen for ages. He left his friends playing ball in the small wood, rolled up his ducks so they didn't get wet, and crossed the brook to where his folks were waiting for him. He found them at the cloister sitting on the bench outside the cell. They were mighty glad to see him again and they sat down together waiting.

The Father Researcher wasn't there. He was kept in the village. He had lots of unfinished business to attend to, lots of work to do.

EPILOGUE

THE RESEARCHER'S BODY WAS NEVER FOUND. He therefore has no tomb. An inquiry the authorities conducted, as they eventually learned he was missing, led to a weird conclusion. The investigators said the researcher, who had been buried under a pile of books, did not try hard enough to get out, and that the books by a mysterious synthesis had swiftly assimilated him without a trace. The explanation seemed partly credible. Some even said it was confirmed by evidence. Fact is, a gang of gypsies climbing up to the library to filch more books and turn them into cornets for their sunflower seeds were scared the hell out of them by a ghost, which they said was haunting Tower B with a black tomcat. The rumor spread rapidly and the gypsies, a superstitious bunch, stopped going there for loot, which was a positive development.

The researcher that had mysteriously disappeared in the tower library was soon forgotten. He was a reclusive man anyway, who didn't make much noise around him and only had few friends. The Researcher Father alone, though burdened with old age, still thinks of him at times and remembers him in his prayers when he prays in his cloister in the woods for those who travel by sea and land and air. He never mentions the researcher's name—perhaps he has forgotten it by now—but still knows very well the story of his life.

Printed in the USA
CPSIA information can be obtained
at www.ICGtesting.com
CBHW032127140424
6922CB00001B/2